It Starts With a Lie

It Starts With a Lie

Mary Clare Lockman

Mary Clare Lockman

ISBN: 978-1946-195081
Library of Congress Control Number: 2017937237
Printed in the United States of America
First Printing 2017

21 20 19 18 17   5 4 3 2 1
Cover Design & Interior Book Design:
FuzionPress

Published by FuzionPress, 1250 E 115th Street,
Burnsville, MN, 55337 USA

To order contact mclockman@msn.com.
Reseller discounts available.

For Ryan, Evan, Cameron, Charlotte, Keira, and Patrick Junior. You'll never know how much joy you bring me. How did I get so lucky? Love, Bumpa

Acknowledgments

Many people help an author bring an idea to fruition. Anne Maylone, my amazing daughter, read all drafts of the book. She gave me valuable feedback and insight. Paul Lockman, my patient husband, listened to me read the entire book aloud to him. To hear the play of the words was very beneficial. Clare Lockman, Erin Elgin, Colleen Holtz, my lovely daughters, have supported me through all my writing projects. Connie Hill, my superb editor, read my final draft. Her gentle suggestions pulled the story together. Lorsie Walseth, my long-time friend, let me use her name, Zastrow, for the second baseman. Her grace and kindness in the face of adversity inspired me. Klaus and Bärbel Musolf, our wonderful friends, let me use their name for the store in Red Wing. Their interest in the book kept me writing. Thank you to all for your encouragement.

A special thank you to Ann Aubitz for her creativity and patience in putting the whole project together.

Chapter One

No More Secrets

I really didn't mean to do it but once it happened I couldn't undo it. I thought it was over but it sure wasn't.

I couldn't tell my mom, dad, Gramps, or even Aunt Florence. Worst of all, I couldn't tell Sally, my best friend since first grade. Sally and I took a pledge three years ago in sixth grade that we would never, ever have secrets from each other.

My mom always said that the more you lie, the more you have to lie. In this case, it was true because I just had to pretend everything was great and fine when it wasn't. What was I going to do?

Chapter Two

Colette

My name is Colette, Colette Antonia McGiver. I live in Red Wing, Minnesota, a town of about 10,000 people on the Mississippi River. I was born on October 12, 1958 so I've lived in Red Wing fourteen and a half years.

I live with my parents, Gemma and John, and my Grandfather, Antonio Rossini. I call him Gramps and he's my favorite person in the world, hands down. He left his family in Italy, went through Ellis Island in 1923, lived and worked in Chicago, met my Grandma Rose, and then moved to Red Wing, where he opened a pharmacy / soda fountain. My dad became partners with Gramps before I was born. Now that Gramps is retired, my dad owns the store.

My mom works at the store part-time and at St. Anastasia's, my grade school, during the school year.

The other member of our family is my mom's sister, Aunt Florence. She's a nursing supervisor at our local hospital. She lives six blocks from our house with her husband, Mike, and their daughter, Rosie.

I'm in the ninth grade at City Bluffs High School and I love it there. My best friend, Sally, goes to the high school too. It was kind of hard for both of us to begin with. We didn't know very many people so Sally and I clung to each other. We had homeroom together and, luckily, we had the same lunch break. So we always had someone to sit with. Now it's the middle of March and Sally and I have made some friends so we have a full table at lunch.

"Colette, you glad basketball's over?" Sheila Donohue asked. Sheila sits at our table every day.

I've played basketball for as long as I can remember. It was a big deal at St. Anastasia's. The whole school and all their families went to the games. Last year, 1972, we actually won the city championship. Gramps cheered and whistled the whole game. We went through every single play as soon as I got home. I knew I could never top that, not in a million years.

Sheila and I were on the high school basketball B-Squad. We played other B-Squads in the area. We had lost our last game against Lake City so the season was over. "I guess I'm glad. Next year I hope I'm on the varsity," I said.

"Me too," Sheila said. "Remember, softball starts in less than two weeks."

"I remember."

We finished eating and Sally pulled me aside. "Can you come over later? I have something to tell you."

"What? Tell me now." Since we never had secrets from each other, I told Sally all my conversations at school and everything that happened at home. She told me everything that happened in her house. It was a lot more exciting than my house, believe me. Sally had five brothers and sisters so the commotion in the house was non-stop.

"I can't right now. It would take too long."

"I'm intrigued." I stepped closer to Sally. "Give me a hint."

"Come over on Saturday."

"It's only Wednesday. I can't wait that long. I have to work on Saturday." I worked every other weekend at our family store making the greatest malts and sodas for our customers. My dad paid me a dollar twenty five cents an hour which was more than I made babysitting. "Should I call you later?"

"No. You know I can't talk for very long. Plus there's no privacy."

The telephone at Sally's house was next to the steps going upstairs. There was a little table for the phone that had a seat attached to it. Mrs. Reynolds yelled at anyone who was on the phone more than ten minutes. Sally's two younger brothers, Joe and Eric, were usually fighting or wrestling each other so loudly that Sally would say, "I can't even think with those two around." If that wasn't enough, Sally's thirteen-year-old sister, Anna, whined about one thing after another. She couldn't use the phone, she didn't get any new clothes, she didn't like the cold, she didn't like the rain, or she didn't even have her own bed; she had to share her bed with eight-year-old Margaret. This brought more yelling from Mrs. Reynolds, who put her hands on her hips, and said, "Would you stop complaining?" At this point Sally would sigh and say, "I better go."

I thought about all those things for a few seconds. "Sal, I guess we'll have to wait until Saturday. I'm going to be thinking about it every minute."

"You won't believe it."

Mrs. Crenshaw was our homeroom teacher and my English teacher too. After lunch, we had ten minutes of homeroom before going to English.

All I could think about was what Sally's secret was.

Everyone left the room except Mrs. Crenshaw's English class. She was nice enough but she sure was a stickler for grammar. You didn't want to say the word ain't in front of her. I pulled out my English book, knowing that we were going to talk about the parts of the sentence again and again. Subjects, direct, and indirect objects were her specialty. And, of course, that led to writing a correct sentence. Our goal for the year was to make sure that we could write a paper that we could be proud of, that she could be proud of, and that our parents could be proud of.

"What is the subject of this sentence?" Mrs. Crenshaw asked. She wrote on the blackboard - Joseph wrote a letter to his wife. "This is review, girls."

Hands went up in the air.

"Joseph," several people said.

"Correct. What's the predicate?" Since predicate was just another word for verb, the hands went up in the air again. "Sam, what's the answer?"

"Wrote," Sam O'Malley said. Sam was short for Samantha. She had long, reddish hair pulled back in a pony tail. Whenever she talked her pony tail moved side to side with a flip of her head. I sat right behind her.

Mrs. Crenshaw paced in front of the class. She was shorter than most of us at five foot two and always dressed perfectly. Everything matched from her scarves to her shoes to her purses. "Okay now, what's the direct object? Remember the predicate acts on the direct object."

"Is it a letter?" Sheila Donohue asked.

"You are correct. That is what Joseph is writing. A letter."

"Now the indirect object. What is it? Colette?"

I looked up from my notebook where I had been doodling. A big question mark with lots of smaller question marks filled the page. I squinted at the board. "Sally," I said.

"I don't see Sally on the board. Try again."

"Secret," I said. I don't know why I said that. It literally flew out of my mouth. It was quiet in the room.

"We have a really interesting sentence, class. Joseph wrote a letter to his secret Sally."

The class laughed.

"I can't top that," Mrs. Crenshaw said. "Let's take out our book, *The Pearl,* and see what John Steinbeck does with his sentences.

Chapter Three

Sally's Secret

I asked Sally Thursday and Friday for a preview. She just smiled. "You'll have to wait until Saturday."

"I hope I can get off early. I'll ask my mom again." If we weren't busy at the store, sometimes I went home at four instead of five.

Friday night at the dinner table I brought it up. "Have you decided about tomorrow?" I looked at my mom.

"About leaving early?"

"Yeah, if it's not busy."

"I think it would be okay for you to leave at four. Only if it's not busy though. Why is it so important?"

"Sally and I have some things to talk about."

"What in the world are you and Sally talking about that's so important?" Gramps asked.

"I don't know."

"Then how do you know it's important?"

"Because she told me it was."

Gramps had a full smile now.   "That's interesting." Gramps took a bite of the tuna and noodle casserole my mom fixed once a month on Fridays. "I'll need to hear everything you discussed with Sally," Gramps said. "Don't leave anything out."

"Sure, Gramps."

Saturday at four o'clock, I walked onto Sally's front porch. She opened the door before I even rang the doorbell. She had gotten her hair cut in the new shag style.

"Cute hair, Sal. Turn around."

Sally fluffed her blond hair as she turned around. "I don't know if I like it."

"I do. You look older."

"Good. Just what I want."

Sally whisked me upstairs to her room. She looked in the closet and even under the bed to make sure no one was hiding. "All clear," she said.

We both plopped down on her double bed. "Well, what happened?" I said.

"Nothing yet," Sally said.

"What do you mean?"

"Well, you know Jake O'Malley?"

"Of course I know Jake O'Malley." Jake was Sam's brother and a junior at our school. He was the star running back on our football team and the star pitcher on our baseball team. If that wasn't enough, he was really, really cute. He had dark brown hair, bright blue eyes, and perfect white teeth that he showed often as he smiled. Sally and I decided shortly after starting high school that he was the cutest boy in the whole school.

"He's been hanging around our house a lot."

"He's friends with John, isn't he?" John was Sally's brother who was two years older than her.

"Yeah, they play baseball together."

"So, what does that have to do with you?"

"I'm just going to blurt it out. He asked me out."

"What?"

"He wants me to meet him at the movie theater."

"Wow, Sally. Tell me exactly what he said."

"Well, he was talking about the movie, *The Poseidon Adventure*. He asked me if I had seen it. I said no, I hadn't. Then he said he was going on Friday and I should go too."

"Are you sure he wants to meet you? Maybe he was just telling you that he wants to see the movie."

"That's not what I heard."

"Are you going?"

"Yeah."

"What did your mom say?"

"Nothing."

"That doesn't sound like your mom."

"I didn't tell her." Sally fluffed up her new hairstyle with her fingers. "She says Jake gives a big smile but he doesn't mean anything he says."

"So she doesn't like him." To tell you the truth, I didn't know how anyone could not like Jake. The boys all wanted to be like him and the girls wanted to be with him.

"My mom says no dating until sixteen. I'm fifteen now and I don't agree." Sally was seven months older than me and had just turned fifteen.

"So what are you going to do?"

"That's where you come in."

"In what way?"

"I may need a cover story. My mom trusts you."

The last person I wanted mad at me was Mrs. Reynolds. Sally had never asked me anything like this before. "If you say you're coming over to my house, that won't work. Our moms talk all the time."

"I know. Please, Colette, help me." Sally's hands were in the praying position. "I may not get another chance with Jake. If I say, wait a year, he'll think I'm a baby."

"I don't know if this is a good idea, Sal."

"Why not?" Sally's blue eyes could look right through you. She waited for me to answer. I didn't have a good answer so I didn't say anything. She continued, "Here's the plan. We can both be dropped off at the movie theater and then we can both be picked up later."

"You mean I'm going with you?"

"I hope so." Her hands were still in the praying position.

"I have wanted to see the movie.

"As long as you're not too close to Jake and me, you can watch the movie too."

"Are you sure about this? It sounds weird to me." I didn't know if she knew what this sounded like. I was supposed to go with her, pretend I wasn't with her at the movie, and then come home with her.

"Jake said next Friday. Does that work for you?"

"I guess." I wasn't sure this was going to work at all.

"Thank you, Colette. Please don't tell anybody."

"Me? Tattle. Never."

"Sally," Mrs. Reynolds yelled.

Sally paid no attention. I guess when you lived in a house with so many people, you tuned out all the noise. I felt a little nervous because Sally was rambling on and on about Jake.

There was a pounding at Sally's door before the door flew open. "Didn't you hear me?" Mrs. Reynolds said with her hands on her hips.

"I don't think I did." Sally said. She looked down at her fingernails. "Did you hear anything, Colette?"

"It doesn't matter what Colette heard or didn't hear. I wasn't calling her. I was calling you," Mrs. Reynolds said. "I need you to babysit while I go to the grocery store. Please come downstairs." Mrs. Reynolds always said please and thank you.

"Isn't John around? It's his turn."

"No, he's not around." Mrs. Reynolds put her hands back on her hips.

Sally got up and said, "I'll be right there."

"Thank you."

"Sal, I'm going to go," I said. It was five o'clock. We hadn't had nearly enough time to talk about her secret plan.

"You can stay and help if you want."

"I better get home." Once in a while I helped Sally babysit. By the time I was done I was grateful for my quiet house and the fact that I had privacy in my bedroom and bathroom.

We walked downstairs. Joe and Eric ran by making their popping sounds as they shot at each other. Anna was already complaining about how mean Sally was going to be to her. Little Margaret waved to me with a big smile.

"Bye, Sal," I said. "I'll let myself out."

Chapter Four

Aunt Florence

My mom's sister, Aunt Florence, lived with us until two and a half years ago. She decided on her thirty seventh birthday she was ready to move into an apartment all by herself. To tell you the truth I thought it was about time but I just smiled and said, "Good luck, Aunt Florence."

Well, one thing led to another, as my mom would say, and Aunt Florence met Mike in her apartment building. He was really nice. He liked Aunt Florence and she liked him so six months later they got married. I was in the wedding and everything. I wore a long, light blue dress and had my thick, wild hair fixed at the hairdresser's. I went to get my hair done with my mom, who was the matron of honor, and Aunt Florence, who was the bride. Then we went to St. Anastasia's Church for the wedding. They took so many pictures that I actually got tired of smiling. I was afraid I was going to wake up the morning after the wedding with a permanent smile on my face.

The reception was at the St. James Hotel and we had a great meal. My mom was so happy she couldn't stop crying the whole day. She said things like "I never thought this would happen" and "She looks so happy." Then she'd burst into tears again.

Aunt Florence did look happy, there was no question about that, and so did Mike. Gramps and my dad got teary a couple of times so I guess I was the only member of the McGiver family who was dry-eyed at Aunt Florence's wedding.

The next thing we knew Aunt Florence announced she was expecting a baby. The tears flowed in the McGiver family again. Gramps kept blowing his nose, wiping his eyes, and saying, "Are you sure?" and "Congratulations." Then he'd pump Mike's hand and hug Aunt Florence.

Anyway, a little more than a year after the wedding, on March sixteenth, little Rosemary Colette was born. It's a date I'll never forget because Aunt Florence and Mike came to my championship basketball game. Aunt Florence yelled, clapped, cheered, and screamed. Well, maybe she was so enthusiastic that her baby decided she wanted to see Aunt Florence for herself. On the way home, Aunt Florence told Mike it was time to go to the hospital. Rosemary Colette was born the day after St. Anastasia won the city championship.

Rosie is cute as can be, especially when she wobbles across the room and everybody claps for her. Then she stops and claps too. So pretty soon the whole house is clapping and smiling. Gramps always has his arms open wide for Rosie. He sweeps her up and says, "How come I'm so lucky that I have a little friend like Rosie?"

I do some babysitting for Aunt Florence and I don't mind for the most part because Rosie is so cute. But the thing that bugs me no end is that whether I babysit for two hours or five hours the payment is always the same – one dollar.

I swore the last time I babysat that was it. I was there from seven o'clock to midnight. Aunt Florence gave me the usual one dollar. I was burning up, believe me. My face was hot. She thought twice about it, I guess. She reached back in her purse and pulled out an extra quarter. Don't be so generous, I thought.

The next morning, I told my mom the story of the dollar twenty five cents. "Anyway, Mom. I'm through. No more babysitting for Aunt Florence."

"I thought you liked little Rosie."

"Of course I like Rosie. She's darling. But I don't like turning down other jobs where I would make more." I needed to make money if I was going to have some of the new clothes I wanted.

"It doesn't hurt you, Colette. You're helping her. And she's family," my mom said.

"I know she's family. That's why I'm doing it."

"She doesn't work as many hours at the hospital as she used to and the house costs too."

"You've told me that before."

"Well, money might be tight."

"Mom, Aunt Florence is cheap. Really cheap."

"Remember, Colette, she's had kind of a sad life."

That was my mom's ace. She wanted me to feel sorry for her sister. Three years ago I found out there were two family secrets. Gramps told me about my Uncle Daniel, who was killed in the Korean War. Evidently, he was Aunt Florence's best friend.

After I heard about Uncle Daniel, Aunt Florence asked me to go to St. Paul with her. We had lunch at the River Room in Dayton's. It was great. Then we went to a place called the Monument where she told me about having a baby when she was eighteen. She named her son, Daniel, and gave him up for adoption. I was shocked, to say the least.

After I got over my shock, I was excited to have a cousin. I wanted to meet him. Aunt Florence contacted the adoption agency and Daniel responded to her letter. They met each other in St. Paul. Then he came to Red Wing to meet the family. Daniel and I discussed basketball and we kind of hit it off. I asked if I could write to him while he studied at the University of Wisconsin in Madison. He said yes so I've written to him for three years. Summer and Christmas vacation he still comes to Red Wing to see Gramps, Aunt Florence, and the rest of us.

I thought over what my mom said about Aunt Florence. "Aunt Florence has Mike and Rosie now so her life isn't so sad."

"That's true. But…"

"No buts. I'm done." I got up from the table. "I thought the past was over. That's what you always tell me."

"We'll have to discuss this later."

"Much later." I left the kitchen. I wasn't getting anywhere with my mom. I didn't like to be rude but I had a lot on my mind right now. Sally's revelation about Jake had certainly given us something to talk about. I hoped Sally knew what she was doing.

Chapter Five

Sally's Date

Sally and I talked all week about her supposed date with Jake. At school, she told him she was going to the movie on Friday night and so was I. He said he'd see her there.

Sally tried fixing her hair differently. There wasn't much you could do with the shag style other than fluff it up a little bit. She asked my opinion over and over. I told her she looked fine. Then I told her she looked great. She finally stopped asking.

The plan was to have Mrs. Reynolds drop Sally and me off at the movie theater at seven o'clock. The movie started at seven thirty. My mom would pick us up at nine forty five. Lots of people at school had seen *The Poseidon Adventure*. Everyone thought it was scary.

My mom dropped me off at Sally's house at six forty five. She talked the whole time in the car about how she couldn't wait for spring to actually be here, how big I was getting, and how she hoped it was a good movie. I didn't have to say a word other than uh huh.

"Bye, Mom," I said. "Thanks for the ride."

"I'll pick you up at nine forty five unless I hear from you. Do you have a dime?"

"I do." My mom always made sure I had a dime for the pay phone in case there was an emergency. I kept it in a separate place in my wallet so I wouldn't spend it.

Sally opened the door as I was walking up the steps to the house. "Colette, hurry up." She rushed me up to her room. "Just a minute." She did her usual search in the closet and under the bed. "All clear," she said.

"Sal, what should I do now?"

"Nothing yet. I'll let you know at the theater. I think you should wait until we decide where we're sitting and then sit in front of Jake and me," Sally said. "And I have to put on my eye shadow in the bathroom."

"Okay." I still wasn't sure about the whole thing but I wanted to be there for my best friend.

"I owe you, Colette. I can't thank you enough." She hugged me tight. "C'mon, let's go. I don't want to be late."

Mrs. Reynolds drove us to the theater. We got our tickets first and then Sally dragged me into the bathroom. She had the bluest eyes so she pulled out some light blue eye shadow. She started to swipe it on. Pretty soon her eyelids were covered with blue powder. "Is this too much?" Sally asked.

To tell you the truth I thought it was a lot but I didn't want to spoil it for her. "I think it's perfect."

"Okay, I'll put this away." Sally put the eye shadow in her purse and pulled out mascara. She flicked at her lashes with the mascara brush. She had long, thick eyelashes but the ends were light. The mascara darkened them up immediately. She reached into her purse and out came some blush. She brushed the pink color under her cheekbones.

"Are you going home like that?"

"No. As soon as the movie is over, I'll come in here and remove the eye makeup and blush." She searched in her purse. Out came a small jar of cold cream. "This is what my mom uses." She set the cold cream carefully in her purse. "One more thing." Sally pulled out red lipstick. It was really red. She outlined her upper lips and her lower lips. She pursed them together, kind of rubbing them back and forth. "Hand me some toilet paper, would you?"

"Here." I handed her a wad of toilet paper.

She took the wad and put it between her lips, then moved her mouth in and out. She looked in the mirror for the tenth time. She fluffed her hair. She made a kissing sound to the mirror. I guess she was ready.

We went back to the lobby. Sally craned her neck as she looked around. I alternated between looking at the popcorn and looking at Sally. No Jake so far.

"Well, we're a little early," Sally said. Sally edged closer to the door. She fidgeted around on one foot, then the other, then back to the first. She reminded me of little Rosie waiting for Gramps to pick her up.

I was starting to think that maybe Jake wasn't going to show up. I bought some popcorn and root beer because the movie started in five minutes. Usually Sally liked to sit in the theater for a while before the movie started. I did too.

I walked over to Sally. "Sal, I'm going into the theater."

"What? You can't."

"Why not? The movie starts in four minutes."

"I know. But you said you'd go with me."

"To the movie. I actually want to see the movie." I walked toward the theater.

"Colette, please." Sally had been staring out the window with her fingers in her mouth.

I turned. I had never had a fight with Sally and I didn't want to now. I decided right then and there that my friendship with her was more important than getting a good seat. "Okay, I'll wait with you," I said. I took a bite of popcorn and a drink of root beer. I looked out the window.

Jake was getting out of his blue 1963 Ford Fairlane. He had his own car which was really unusual. He sauntered over and opened the lobby door. No hurry, I guess. Sally had a look on her face I had never seen before. It was a cross between relief and adoration.

"Hi, Sally," Jake said. "Should we get some popcorn and pop?" He nodded toward me.

"The movie has already started," I said.

Neither one of them said anything. They went over to the counter to order the popcorn. Sally was giggling happily every time Jake looked at her. I heard him say, "How about a bucket of popcorn and two glasses of pop?"

"Whatever you say," Sally said.

"Oh, there's Mike." Jake waved his hand. "Over here," he yelled.

Mike walked over and said, "Hey, man." Sally looked puzzled by the presence of Mike. She stood right next to Jake.

I guess no one but me cared that the movie had started. I was trying to be patient but since I'm not the most patient person in the world, it was more than hard. Hopefully, the previews were still running so we wouldn't miss the beginning of the movie. I had no idea where I was going to sit. The good seats in the middle were probably taken. If there were any left, I'd have to crawl over people and they didn't like that. I didn't either. It was embarrassing.

Sally walked away from me. "Aren't you going to come, Colette? Hurry up," she twittered.

There was no point in saying anything. Sally had already turned away from me. I wouldn't make a scene in public so I just tagged along behind like a puppy dog. We walked into the theater and it was really dark. An ad was running about getting popcorn, candy, and pop and then putting the trash in a wastebasket. That meant the previews of other movies were already finished. The next thing was the movie itself.

Jake was unconcerned about all the people staring at us as we tried to find seats. He pointed to a space with two seats along the side. I stood in the aisle holding my popcorn and pop.

The movie started.

"Would you sit down?" Someone said.

"Or leave," someone else barked.

"SHH," many people said.

"Mike, why don't you sit here with Sally," Jake said. "C'mon, Colette, I'll go with you."

I didn't have time to react since I felt the whole theater was looking at us. I walked up to the front, my least favorite spot, and saw two seats right in the middle. I said, "Excuse me. Excuse me." I sat down. I leaned over to put my pop under my seat and my popcorn spilled all over the man next to me. He jumped up to brush the popcorn on the floor. "I don't believe you," he said. "Why don't you come on time?"

"Will you be quiet?" A woman behind us said.

"Shut up," several people snarled.

I heard the crunch of popcorn being stepped on. I wanted to crawl in a hole but I didn't dare move. There would be a riot and then the police would be escorting me outside. Best to get as small as possible. I scrunched down in my seat.

Jake sat down next to me on the other side but not before he said, "Relax, everybody."

He sure had a lot of confidence in himself. I had to admit that I liked him sitting next to me. After all, he was the cutest boy in the school and a great left-handed pitcher. I wondered what Sally was doing with Mike.

I didn't wonder for long because the movie was really interesting. People were in the dining room of the ship, SS Poseidon, celebrating New Year's Eve. The scene changed to the captain talking on the phone. He was being warned about a huge wave. The wave filled the screen and hit the ship. The whole ship turned upside down. It was really scary. The people who were still alive had to swim to the top which was really the bottom. Only six were rescued. I was exhausted by the end of the movie.

I decided right then and there that I would never take a ship across the ocean. In fact, I was glad we lived nowhere near an ocean. Minnesota was in the perfect spot.

"Good movie, huh?" Jake said.

"Yeah, it was great," I said. I started walking toward the aisle. Jake stopped me.

"Colette, I want to ask you something."

"Okay."

"I'm looking for a job. Could you tell your dad that?"

"That you're looking for a job?"

"No, that I'd like to work at your store."

"I don't know if he needs anyone."

"What about stocking? I've done that at night at the grocery store."

"I don't know."

"Can you ask him? You won't regret it." Jake flashed his smile at me.

I stood in the aisle, trying to see Sally but there were too many people. Jake was behind me.

"I've got to catch up with Mike. Bye, Colette." Jake said. He pushed his way through the crowd, saying "Excuse me."

To tell you the truth, I wasn't in any hurry. A lot of people knew I was the one who had been late and caused the ruckus. I wasn't about to push and shove my way. Anyway,

Sally was going to pelt me with questions the minute she saw me.

Sally had her hands on her hips. Jake was nowhere to be seen and neither was Mike. I had known Sally for as long as I could remember. I knew a mad face when I saw one.

"Hi, Sal," I said. "Wasn't the movie great? I sure don't want to go on a ship soon. Or ever. I'm glad…"

"What are you glad about? That you were sitting with Jake?" Sally snapped the words one after another.

"No. I was going to say I was glad I live in Minnesota. Away from the ocean." I couldn't say I was glad I sat next to Jake but I wasn't sad either. Maybe she would drop it since it really wasn't my fault.

"Did you tell him to sit next to you?"

"You were right there. He's the one who sat next to me." I wanted to move out of the aisle because people were looking at us again.

"This was my date and you wrecked it," Sally said. Her eyes narrowed until all I saw was her light blue eye shadow.

"What?"

"Just what I said. I saw you talking when the lights came up."

"He was asking me something."

"Did you set up another date with him?"

"No, I wasn't on a date with him. And I don't want to date him. If you want to know the truth, he asked me if my dad was hiring at the store."

"I don't believe you." Her fists were so tight at her thighs that I could see white knuckles.

"It's the truth."

"Then why were you smiling at each other?"

Of course, he was smiling. He always did. And of course, I smiled back. It would have been impossible not to with his perfect white teeth and all. "I didn't know I was smiling." My face felt hot. Oh no. I hoped I wasn't blushing. Sally told me I blushed more easily than anyone she knew. I blamed it on my wild, reddish-brown hair and white skin.

"That's all I need to know," Sally said. We were out of the movie theater and Sally headed to the bathroom. I started to go in with her. "I thought you were my best friend, Colette. Please don't come in here with me."

I stood open-mouthed. I hoped my mom would be on time because I was getting nervous. I really didn't know what I had done.

Sally stomped out of the bathroom. Her eye makeup was gone, as was the blush on her cheeks. There was a little lipstick left on her bottom lip but I didn't dare say anything. She broke the silence. "You're not going to apologize, are you?"

"For what?"

"For stealing my date."

"I wasn't on a date with Jake. He's the one who sat by me." I wanted to say, you made me come with you and lie to your mom. Then it wasn't what you imagined.

"Right. I'm going to look for your mom," Sally said. "By the way, Colette, please don't call me this weekend."

I didn't say a word. I was too worn out.

Thankfully, my mom was there. We got in the car and my mom had a million questions about the movie. She wondered if she should see it with my dad. I said yes, it was exciting. She asked Sally if she liked it and Sally said yes. I felt Sally staring at me in the dark. I felt my face getting hot again.

"Anyway, Mom, I'm so glad Gramps came all the way to Minnesota."

"I am too but why are you saying that?"

"Because we don't live by the ocean."

My mom laughed. "It sounds like a pretty scary movie."

We dropped off Sally who said, "Thank you, Mrs. McGiver." She slammed the door of the car and hurried up the steps of her house.

"You can move to the front seat, if you want," my mom said.

I was still reeling from the events of the night. The slammed door rang in my ears. "No thanks."

"Sally was awfully quiet. Didn't she like the movie?"

"She liked the movie but she was really tired."

"Oh. She seemed tired."

Dad and Gramps asked me all about the movie. I begged off after a while, saying I wanted to go to bed. I lay in bed, with the lights off. I didn't want anyone to know I was still awake. I couldn't figure out what happened between Sally and me. After all, I said I'd help her with her problem and then she got mad at me. It was the worst night of my life.

And, I had to admit that Jake was really nice to me. I liked sitting next to him. I was going to ask my dad if he needed any help in the store. Maybe he'd hire Jake. Then I could see him all the time. That might make the whole night worth it.

Chapter Six

Musolf's

I must have been really worn out from the night before because I didn't even wake up until eleven o'clock. Since basketball season was over, I couldn't go up to the gym to practice. What was I going to do? I wanted to go over to Sally's but she had made it clear not to even call her. I wasn't going to beg, believe me. Hopefully, the whole thing would just blow over.

I knew Gramps would be downstairs but since it was eleven already, he would have finished breakfast, gotten dressed, done some reading, gone for a walk, and maybe even gone to Mass. Sometimes Gramps liked to go to Mass on other days than Sundays but not me. Sunday was enough for the whole week.

I walked downstairs and checked in the kitchen. Gramps wasn't there. I looked in the sunroom and there he was hunched over the desk, paying some bills. Gramps prided himself on never paying a bill late.

"Hi, Gramps," I said.

"Hi." Gramps looked up. "I want to hear more about the movie. Do you have some time?"

"Sure." I had all the time in the world. "It was great. I thought about you taking a ship from Italy. Was it scary?"

"Yes, it was kind of scary. Partly because I left my whole family. I didn't know if I'd ever see them again. And the ship made all kinds of creaking sounds, especially at night. Nighttime was the worst."

"I'm glad you didn't turn upside down."

"I am too because I never learned to swim. What are you doing today?"

"I think I'll ride my bike around and maybe go down to the store."

"Okay, I'll see you later, then.

Main Street in Red Wing was wonderful. People strolled along the sidewalks, looking in all the different shops. On weekends in the summer, it was literally crazy with visitors driving from St. Paul or elsewhere. People liked the famous Red Wing Pottery but everyone wanted to look in Red Wing Shoes, where the giant leather boot stood. I liked it myself, even though I'd seen it a million times.

I was standing in front of Musolf's, the store everybody in Red Wing loved. It was like a general store with amazing new merchandise every week. I could spend the whole day in there, believe me.

Anyway, Jake and his friend, Mike, saw me standing there. John, Sally's brother, was right behind Jake. He nodded but Jake stopped to talk to me. I couldn't believe my luck.

"Colette, c'mon in with us," Jake said.

How could I say no to that? "Sure," I said.

I walked into Musolf's with Jake, John, and Mike. Tommy Musolf was behind the counter at the cash register. He was a year older than me but we were friends. His dad, Fred, owned the store and he was friends with my dad. Tommy's grandfather was great friends with Gramps. His grandmother had been friends with my grandmother. Everybody in town called Tommy's grandmother, Oma.

Tommy's grandfather and grandmother started the family business just like Gramps had started ours with Grandma Rose. My mom said that Gramps and Grandpa Musolf really understood each other since they had both left their countries and started new lives in Red Wing, Minnesota. So our whole family was friends with their whole family.

I stopped at the cash register. "Hi, Tommy," I said. "How's it going?"

"Good. Baseball starts next week. I'm going to try out for the varsity team this year. How about you? You gonna play softball?"

"I played last summer. I loved it. I can play on the B-Squad this year." I looked around. Jake, Mike, and John were nowhere to be seen.

"Colette, are you with Jake O'Malley?" Tommy's arms were crossed over his chest.

"No."

"It seemed like you came in with them."

"Oh, that. They were walking in at the same time I was." It wasn't like I met them in front of the store on purpose. It just happened. I looked around. "Tommy, see you later."

I found John near the back of the store. He said, "Colette, maybe you should go home."

"Why?"

"Just go home." He walked away.

I should have. I really should have.

I didn't want to leave without saying good bye to Jake. I walked down the aisle moving my head from left to right. He leaned against the wall reading a comic book. I walked over. "Hi," I said.

"Hi, Colette." Jake bumped into me. I almost fainted. "Sorry. Oh, I've got to find Mike." He walked away and then turned around. "Meet us outside."

I didn't move for a full minute. I had no idea why he wanted me to meet them. Maybe it had something to do with wanting to work at our store. I thought about Sally, fuming away at home.

"C'mon." Jake and Mike swaggered past me. I followed.

"Bye, Tommy," I said. I waved.

"We have to move around the corner," Jake said. "Into the alley."

"Colette should leave," John said.

"I've got it handled," Jake said. He winked at me. "Okay, empty your pockets."

I should have run as fast as I could. But I was curious about why we were standing at the entrance to an alley. I didn't have to wonder for long. John pulled out several batteries from one of his pockets. I stared. Mike had candy bars, three in each pocket. He held them up. I stared. "Look at this," Jake said. He had a pack of cigarettes. I couldn't believe it. Then he reached into his other pocket and out came a lighter. He flicked it and the little flame danced.

"You're stealing," I said. "I'm going to tell Tommy." I started walking back to Musolf's.

Jake blocked my way. "Check your coat pockets, Colette."

"Why?"

"Just check."

I pulled out a candy bar. "What? I didn't take this."

"Really? It was in your pocket. Maybe I'll go tell your friend, Tommy, that you stole from him."

I remembered Jake bumping into me in the store. I couldn't stand Tommy, his dad, or his grandparents thinking I had stolen from them. "I won't forget this," I said.

"I'm sure you won't." Jake grabbed a candy bar from Mike and took a big bite.

"You should all be ashamed of yourselves," I yelled.

"Oh, we are," Jake said. "Aren't we boys?"

"Yeah," Mike and John said together.

"I'm going home," I said.

"Mum's the word," Jake said. He held his finger to his mouth. "Our little secret."

I couldn't look at any of them. All I wanted to do was go home. I ran to where my bike was parked in front of Musolf's. I felt the candy bar in my pocket. Should I tell Tommy? I had to think about it. I got on my bike and began to pedal.

It had been quite a day. I reached into my pocket and found the candy bar. I felt it and then I did something strange. My mouth started watering and all I could think about was the candy bar in my pocket. I took it out and looked at it. I thought I better do something with it before I got home. I guess I didn't think for too long because pretty soon the chocolate was melting in my mouth. I had no trouble finishing it before I parked my bike in the garage and walked into my house.

Chapter Seven
Bitter Chocolate

The very worst thing that could have happened, happened right then. I heard Tommy Musolf's grandfather talking in his animated way. I knew I couldn't sneak by the sunroom because the back door was right by it. Instead, I walked into the room and kissed Gramps on the cheek. Gramps and Mr. Musolf both smiled from ear to ear when they saw me.

"Hi, Colette," Mr. Musolf said. He stood up and gave me a hug. He motioned for me to sit.

"Hi, Mr. Musolf," I said. I almost choked on my words. I didn't say I just saw Tommy or I know people who stole from your store. I just stood there and said nothing more. My face felt hot.

"Sit down, Colette," Gramps said. He pointed to my favorite chair. It was a big chair that I literally sunk into.

Plus, the sun was always shining on the chair so the person sitting there was warm inside and out. As tempting as it was to let myself sink in and talk to two of my favorite people I said, "No thanks, Gramps." He looked puzzled. I quickly added, "I have to use the bathroom."

Gramp's eyebrows went up and stayed there arched over his black eyes. "You better go then," he said.

I didn't exactly run up the stairs but I sure wanted to. I went into the bathroom, looked at my red face in the mirror, and took out my toothbrush. I brushed, rinsed, brushed again, and rinsed again. The taste of chocolate was strong in my mouth.

Then, contrary to my whole personality, I stayed upstairs. I put on a Beatles record. I lay on my bed and stared at the ceiling.

I heard a loud knock at my door before my mom came in. "It's four o'clock," she said.

"Oh, I must have fallen asleep." I jumped up to make sure my record player had shut off. I slid the record back in its jacket and closed the lid of the record player. I put the record on the shelf underneath.

"You aren't sick, are you?"

"No, I'm not sick. How come you're home already?"

"We weren't busy, so I came home." My mom felt my forehead. "No temp," she said.

It was funny because even though I didn't have a temp, I felt like I had the flu. Everything ached. "Did Sally call?"

"No, I don't think so."

"Ask Gramps, would you?"

"Did you and Sally have a fight?"

"No. What makes you think that?"

"I don't know. She was awfully quiet last night. And she slammed the door when she left the car."

I didn't say anything because I didn't want to talk about the movie and Sally's weird behavior. I certainly didn't want to talk about what happened at Musolf's store. I swallowed. "I do have some homework, Mom."

My mom stared at me hard. "Okay, you know you can talk to me about anything that's bothering you, don't you?"

"Yes, Mom. I do and I will." Actually, I had no intention of talking to my mom. If I told her about Sally's supposed date and what we did to fool Mrs. Reynolds, she would have been mad at me and then told Mrs. Reynolds. And Sally would never talk to me again, believe me. Best to keep my mouth shut. I could accidentally spill the beans if I started talking. "Are we having hamburgers tonight?"

"Our usual Saturday night dinner."

"Good. I can't wait."

"See you later." My mom walked out of the room.

That night at dinner, Gramps talked non-stop. It was nothing new after Mr. Musolf had been there for a visit. "I thought Colette would come back to chat with us." he said.

"I wanted to, Gramps. I fell asleep." I took one of my mom's homemade french fries and dipped it in ketchup. It was really good. "I suppose you talked about the old country."

"We did. We talked about all the people we left." I had looked at maps with Gramps and Mr. Musolf many times. Mr. Musolf showed me the town he grew up in. It had been part of East Prussia. After World War Two the town became part of Poland. We always looked at Caserta, Italy. Gramps was born on a farm not too far from the town.

Gramps had a sister named Sofia who still lived near Caserta in Italy. Her four children and seven grandchildren all lived nearby. We had gone there to visit two years ago at Christmas. It was wonderful. We saw all the places Gramps had talked about; his family home on the farm, his school, the beautiful piazza in Caserta, and the place in Naples where his ship left from.

I couldn't talk to Aunt Sofia's family because I didn't speak Italian so I kept Gramps close by. He didn't mind so I was his little shadow the whole time we were in Italy.

Aunt Sofia, her daughter, and three of her grandchildren came from Italy last summer to visit us. Gramps was excited to show his family Red Wing and our family store. We drove to Lake Pepin, searching for eagles. We saw the paddle wheelers and other boats on the river. We walked up and down Main Street many times. Aunt Florence and her family liked the Fourth of July fireworks the best.

"Anyway, now that basketball is over, I can't wait for softball," Gramps said.

"I can't either." I had played fast pitch softball the summer before. I loved it. I especially loved picking up a hot grounder, throwing it to first base, and getting the batter out. I played shortstop or third base so there was a lot of action. If I hit a single, I'd look at the stands. Gramps would be cheering just like he did at the basketball games.

"When do you start practice?"

"The beginning of April. We're inside to begin with depending on the weather. We'll probably play a lot of catch."

"How many games do you have?"

"Eight and hopefully a championship game. It's a short season."

"You need a good pitcher for fast pitch," my dad said.

"Sam O'Malley is a really good pitcher. Remember, I played with her last summer?"

"I remember her," Gramps said. "She has reddish hair and could she throw the ball. It was fun to watch her."

"I was glad I didn't have to hit against her."

"By the way, Colette, you never told me what you and Sally talked about last weekend."

"It wasn't all that interesting, to tell you the truth."

"I might find it interesting."

This was completely unlike Gramps. If I said no or didn't want to talk, he left me alone. Maybe it had something to do with the fact that I didn't talk to him and Mr. Musolf. Now all eyes were on me. I had to think fast.

"Well, let's see. We talked about how we were going to get to the movie. We had to ask Mrs. Reynolds to drive one way. She said she'd drop us off. We talked about how we were going to get home. I said I'd talk to my mom about picking us up. Then Sally's little sister, Margaret, was in the room for a while so we talked about St. Anastasia's and our old teachers with her. I told her I hoped she didn't get Mrs. Bosworth because she didn't let up for the whole year. And then...

"Okay, I get the picture. We used to call it girl talk."

"That's what it was, Gramps. Lots of boring girl talk."

Chapter Eight
Sundays

Sunday was Gramp's favorite day of the week. He liked to start the week off right, he always said, with Mass and breakfast at the Diner. He dressed in his best suit, a tie, a vest, shiny black shoes, and a hat. He had a round, silver watch on a chain that fit right in his vest pocket. He always wore a long-sleeved white shirt with cufflinks that had an A on them. The A stood for Antonio and my Grandma Rose had given them to him. So he brought all his thoughts about Grandma Rose with him to church where he prayed and sang to his heart's delight.

I couldn't say I felt the same way as Gramps about church but at least I didn't have to wear a dress. My mom said I could wear pants as long as they weren't jeans and no shorts in the summer. I didn't argue, believe me, or I'd be right back to wearing a dress even during the winter.

My dad loved Sundays because the store was closed all day. He said he could concentrate on his family and that was his favorite thing. He dressed in a suit and my mom always dressed in a dress. They held hands as we walked the six blocks to church. I asked every other week if we could ride in the car but my dad said it was good for us to get some exercise. The only time we rode was if it was pouring rain or really cold.

I hoped to see Sally at Mass since the whole Reynolds family went every week. We went into the church and walked down the center aisle. Gramps genuflected before going into the pew. I sat down next to Gramps. Sally's family was about five rows in front of us. Good. I was ready to wave back if Sally turned around and waved.

Gramps opened his missal. He had skinny ribbons marking certain places so he had no problem finding the right page. Father Walsh came out and everyone stood up. Mass started. From then on we stood, sat, knelt, stood, sat, and knelt as prayers were recited and songs were sung.

I had trouble paying attention to Father Walsh and the whole Mass for that matter. All I thought about was that Sally was still mad at me. She was the person I never hesitated pouring my heart out to. Since I didn't have a sister or a brother, I was so happy I had Sally. She was my best friend.

Today, Joe and Eric were on their best behavior. They stood and sat quietly the whole time. After Mass, my mom and Mrs. Reynolds chatted in the back of the church. Sally was more interested in her fingernail polish than in talking with me. I tried to start a conversation several times but after getting one word answers from Sally, I gave up. I stood there looking at my fingernails even though they didn't have any polish on them.

"Did you and Sally have a falling out?" My mom asked as we walked home.

"I really don't know but she seems mad about something."

"What could she be mad about?"

"Like I said, I don't know." I wished my mom would stop with all the questions.

"Did something happen at the movie?"

I couldn't very well say that Sally thought I took her date away from her. And that we had lied to both our moms. I wondered how I got caught up in the whole thing. "Not that I know of," I said.

"Well, here's something that has worked really well for me. All through the years. It doesn't hurt to apologize in case you hurt someone's feelings even if you didn't mean to." My mom was being really sincere.

I had to admit no one ever seemed to be mad at my mom so maybe it worked for her. I actually thought Sally should apologize to me. For many things, if you want to know the truth. If I had said no to begin with about being her alibi, she would have been mad at me. I went along with her and she still was mad at me. I wouldn't be apologizing anytime soon. "I'll think about it, Mom. I really will."

We went to the Diner for breakfast like we did almost every week. Gramps had pancakes every week. I had bacon and eggs with hash browns every week. I took a bite of my bacon. It was delicious.

"How do you practice softball inside?" My dad asked.

"We'll play catch and field grounders. The pitchers practice too but we won't hit. I suppose Coach Richter will have us running back and forth in the gym." I ate a forkful of hash browns.

"That's good. It gets you in shape for running the bases.

Gramps spread his butter on a pancake. It had to be on every square inch of the pancake before he put the syrup on it.

"What are you doing this afternoon?" My mom asked.

"I don't have anything planned."

"I'm going to walk down by the river," my dad said. My dad loved the Mississippi River. It was one of the reasons why Red Wing was where it was, he always said. Over the decades, Red Wing had shipped tons of grain from its port. The river was pretty cool, I had to admit. There were sailboats, barges, speedboats, and of course, paddle wheelers. Some of the boats went all the way down to New Orleans. I guess I loved it too.

"Maybe I'll come with you," I said.

Chapter Nine
Stealing is Fun

After spending almost two weeks in the gym playing catch and picking up grounders, we were all anxious to be outside. Everyone who tried out for the B-Squad made it so I didn't have to worry about being cut.   Coach Richter had decided who would be in the infield and outfield. We had four girls trying out for pitcher. Sam O'Malley was so much better than the rest of them that two dropped out immediately. The coach said it was perfect to have two pitchers.

The second week in April, we went outside to the ball field behind the school. "You can't play the game if you don't know the rules," Coach Richter said. He was a real stickler for the rules. So he would fire questions at us about things like where to throw the ball, how to run through first base or round it, and how to bunt to get on base. And, of course, fast pitch was different than slow pitch because the runner could steal.

"We play heads up ball," he said. "Let's suppose that you get on first base and you feel pretty good about that. Wouldn't you would feel much better if you were on second base and in scoring position if someone hits the ball into the outfield?"

We all looked at each other, nodded, and said, "Yes."

"Okay, good. When can you steal?"

"When you're on first or second base." Sam O'Malley said.

"Yes, but I mean when can you leave the bases?"

"After the pitcher lets go of the ball," I said.

"Excellent, McGiver. When the pitcher releases the ball."

"Do you give the signal?" Sheila Donahue asked.

"I do. I'll be the third base coach when you're up at bat. When I touch the side of my nose, go on the next pitch." The coach touched the left side of his nose and then made a fast, forward motion with his right hand. "We're going to try it right now. I need infielders and no outfielders. Who wants to try third base?"

No one raised their hand. "I will, Coach," I said.

He nodded. I ran to third with my glove.

"Shortstop?" Several girls raised their hands. "Pearson," he said.

"Second base?" He looked around the group. "Okay, Zastrow."

"First? Donahue, go."

"The outfielders are going to be the runners. The other infielders go to a spot and wait your turn for a grounder. We need a catcher." Suzy Malone was playing softball for the first time. She had really worked on catching during our inside practices. She ran behind the coach.

"I'll hit grounders and then the runners will go. Try to get them out. If they get on base, the pitcher will throw to Malone and the batter will try to steal second." He looked around the bases. "Everybody, ready? Oh, and Malone, try to throw them out at second if you can."

I got ready. My glove was down. The grounder came sharply down the third base line. I scooped it up and threw to first. The batter was out. I went behind the other two girls waiting at third.

The coach hit to Pearson at short. She bobbled the ball a little before she threw to first so the runner was safe. The coach touched the left side of his nose. Sam swung her right hand back with the ball in it up over her shoulder. Her arm came down and then accelerated in a quick, windmill motion. She released the ball and it rocketed toward home. It was amazing. The runner on first was off, trying to steal second. The ball sailed right over home plate into Malone's glove. Poor Malone, she got all flustered and threw the ball toward second. Zastrow was waiting with her glove out. Well, the ball went between second and shortstop and right into the outfield on the fly. Malone put her hand up to her mouth and said, "I didn't know I could throw it that far."

"Straighten out your throw and you've got the runner out," Coach Richter said.

Next we worked on double plays. Coach Richter hit me a grounder and I threw it to second. Laurie Zastrow was a master of the double play. She snagged the ball out of the air, touched second base, and threw it to first. It seemed like one motion.

"That was fantastic," the coach said. He hit grounders around the infield. When Zastrow fielded a grounder, Pearson was waiting at second base. She touched the base and threw the ball quickly to first. No problem.

We worked on grounders and stealing for a while and all of us got a chance to run and steal second. Then the coach called all the infielders in and hit some pop flies to the outfielders.

"We still have to have hitting practice. Everyone gets five hits and you run on the last one."

And so our first practice outside finished. "Good job, everyone. Tomorrow, same place. Remember, our first game is only two weeks away. We'll play every Monday and some weeks we'll play on Wednesday too." We had to get in eight games before June ninth, the date of the championship against Lake City.

I went over to the bench to pick up my jacket and there was Sally walking over toward me. Oh good, I thought.

She waved and I waved back. "Hi, Sam," she said. Sam was right behind me waving to Sally.

"Do you want to go get an ice cream cone?" Sam said. There was an ice cream shop across from the school that we liked to go to.

"Sure," Sally said.

"I could use an ice cream cone," I said.

"Don't you have to be home, Colette?"

"Not for a while."

"Oh, I think you do. You don't want to be late." Sally looked at me the same way she always looked at her sister, Anna. Her eyebrows were knit together and her lips were nothing more than a thin, straight line. She walked away from me. "C'mon, Sam, I've got a full hour before I have to be home."

I stood there while they walked away from me. Sam looked back and shrugged her shoulders but Sally looked straight ahead all the way.

I talked about practice at the dinner table and Gramps loved the idea of stealing bases. No one had asked me about Sally for a week. I guess they all figured Sally and I had had a fight and we'd get over it sometime. From what I saw today, Sally was going to continue to blame me for a long time. And so at this time in my life, I didn't have a best friend.

I thought of something. "Hey, Dad, do you need anyone to help stock at the store?"

"We probably should hire someone else. When the pharmacy is busy, I can't do anything else. It's too much for your mother to stock the shelves, take care of the register, and relieve the person making malts."

"I know of a person looking for a job," I said. I hadn't seen Jake since the day at Musolf's.

"I think it's a good idea," my dad said. "What's his name?"

"Jake O'Malley."

"Is he sixteen?"

"Yes."

"Tell him to stop by after school and we can talk."

"I will, Dad. Thanks."

Chapter Ten

Changing Tables

I decided I'd get to school just as the bell rang to avoid standing there while Sally looked at her nails. We filed in for homeroom and there was Sally making sure she didn't look at me. I didn't know how long this was going to go on but today I wanted to scream, "I didn't do anything."

It wasn't like I didn't have any other friends but it was hard to change my routine. Sally and I did things with other girls and then the two of us discussed what so and so said and what so and so did. My mom had been saying things recently like, "Don't put all your eggs in one basket." I guess she meant that I should try to make new friends.

At lunchtime, we sat at a long table with about ten of us. Sally sat at the end of the table so she didn't have to sit next to me. Today she was laughing uproariously with Sam

O'Malley. I wondered what was so funny. I looked over at the table next to us and there was Suzy from my softball team. I had never sat at that table but there was an open seat and some of the other girls were also on my softball team.

I stood up and walked to the other table. "Hi, Suzy. Can I join you?"

Suzy looked surprised but didn't hesitate. "Sure. Here's a place." She patted the open spot.

"Thanks." I sat down next to Suzy. Laurie Zastrow and Mary Pearson were across from me. They both said, "Hi." I could still hear Sally's loud laughing.

"I'm glad you came over, Colette, because I wanted to ask you some questions about softball." Suzy took a bite out of her apple. "I'm really new to it and I don't know all the rules."

"I played last year in the summer but I don't know everything either. You have to listen to the coach."

"You always know where to throw the ball. I get so nervous sometimes. Then I throw it and the girl's already on the base or the throw's nowhere near the base."

Suzy was right. She really could catch the ball but sometimes her throws had nothing to do with what was going on in the game. I could be standing there by third base with the runner already there and here comes a wild throw from Suzy. "Well, if the runner is at the base or you know you can't get her out, throw it back to the pitcher."

"I'll work on that tonight at practice. I do like catching."

"You'll get better at the throwing. Sam isn't easy to catch and you have no problem with that." After a while I forgot that I was sitting at a different table and I started to enjoy it. Suzy talked me up to the other girls and pretended that I knew everything there was to know about softball. I decided right then and there that I was not going to sit at the end of my old table hoping someone talked to me or looked at me. I finished my lunch and got up to leave. "Can I join you again tomorrow?"

"Of course, Colette," Suzy said. "I was hoping you'd say that."

"Good. I'll see you tomorrow." I walked out of the lunchroom and didn't even glance in Sally's direction. I didn't care what she thought.

I had to go to my locker for a minute before I went to homeroom. Down the hall with a couple of junior girls was Jake. The girls laughed at whatever he said. One of them tossed her long hair to the side and then fluffed it up with her fingers all while leaning forward toward Jake. Jake saw me. He came right over to my locker.

"Colette, did you talk to your dad?" Jake asked. "You know, about a job?"

"I did last night. He said to stop over at the store and he'll talk to you."

"Thanks, Colette. I can't thank you enough. Gotta go." He hustled off.

I noticed the girls who had been hanging on Jake's movements and gestures had their hands on their hips. I suppose it bugged them that they had been laughing and enjoying themselves and Jake left to talk to me. If that wasn't enough, there was Sally standing with her chin on her chest. She looked like she was going to come over to question me so I closed my locker and went into my homeroom.

I got my books ready for English class. We had finished *The Pearl* and now were reading *To Kill a Mockingbird*. I liked the book but Mrs. Crenshaw loved the book so she was always pointing out secret meanings and themes within the book. I didn't know how she knew that that's what the author meant but Mrs. Crenshaw was very sure of herself when it came to books.

Anyway, I saw Sally's shoes go by and I didn't look up. I was just too busy getting ready for my afternoon classes.

At practice, Suzy came over to ask me some more questions. I told her I was exactly like her a year ago and I learned by playing.

Suzy said, "Really. I can't believe it. You're so confident. Thanks for helping me."

"Sure. It's all part of being on a team. We help each other."

Coach Richter hit the infielders ground balls as usual. We had to field three each. He hit fly balls to the outfield and pop-ups to the infield. Batting practice consisted of five hits each and running on the last one. Sam and the other pitcher pitched to us. Sam was not throwing her hardest but she was still hard to hit. I was glad she was on our team.

"Okay, girls, we're done until tomorrow," Coach Richter said. "I'll tell you by the end of the week who's starting for our first game and at what position. Everyone will get a chance to play."

"Thanks, Coach," I said. I biked home from practice.

Dinner was almost ready when I got home. I had been coming home and then going right up to my room since Sally got mad at me. I didn't want to answer any questions. I felt different today because softball was really fun and I was going to sit with Suzy at lunch tomorrow. Also, I had talked to Jake at school, much to the chagrin of Sally and others.

"Hi, Mom," I said. My mom was in the kitchen putting the finishing touches on dinner. She spooned the steaming mashed potatoes into a bowl.

"Hi. How was school and practice?"

"Good. They were both good."

If my mom was surprised by my good mood, she didn't show it. She was too busy putting butter on top of the potatoes in various places. The butter started melting immediately so there were little puddles of yellow on top of the white potatoes. She shook some paprika over all of it.

"Should I take this to the table?"

"Thanks, Colette."

We all sat down and Gramps said "Grace." "Bless us oh Lord..." he started. We all joined in. "Thank you, Lord, for our food and for our family," he added.

"Colette," my dad said, "I had an interesting visitor this afternoon."

"Who?"

"Your friend, Jake, came by. He said he's looking for a job and he's willing to do anything. He said he'd run prescriptions to people's houses and stock the shelves. That would really help me."

Wow. I didn't think he would go in there right away. "Sounds good, Dad. Are you going to hire him?"

"I told him I'd think about it and get back to him. What do you think? Is he trustworthy?"

"Yes and he's hard-working too." Actually, I didn't know that but he sure wanted a job. For some reason, I had put the incident at Musolf's out of my mind. Maybe they had forgotten to pay. Yes, that was it. I took a bite of the buttery mashed potatoes.

"Okay. I'll call him and let him know that he's got the job."

Chapter Eleven

Saturday at the Store

The next day at school, I felt light in every way. The things that made me feel sad like Sally not speaking to me and sitting at a lunch table where the people didn't want me were gone. I couldn't say that I didn't care about Sally's behavior but I had a nice group of girls who wanted me to sit with them. Sally could ignore me all she wanted.

I walked into homeroom and sat down at my desk. I put the books I needed for my morning classes on top of the desk.

"That was fun at lunch yesterday, Colette," Suzy said. She stood in the aisle next to me with a little smile and waited.

"It was," I said. It was a funny thing but I didn't remember that Suzy was in my homeroom. I guess I had always been so busy with Sally that I didn't even pay attention to the other girls.

Sally came up behind Suzy and stood there. I was just going to say hi when she harrumphed. I turned toward Suzy. "I'm looking forward to lunch today, Suzy," I said.

Sally's mouth became much thinner. She had a temper but who wouldn't with all the stuff that went on at her house. She used to say she had to stick up for herself or she would disappear in her family because they were all so strong-willed. Sally fit right in because she was one of the most stubborn people I had ever met. I had liked that she wouldn't give in once she set her mind to something. Now, as I looked at her out of the corner of my eye, I didn't think it was such a great trait to have. Just how long can you stay mad at somebody?

Sam O'Malley walked into the room and I tell you, Sally immediately glued herself to Sam. Whoosh. Sally couldn't have been any closer to her if she had tried. She actually put her arm around Sam and guffawed. The whole class heard her.

"Everyone, take your seats," Mrs. Crenshaw said. I was already sitting so I looked straight ahead at the teacher. "We have next week off for Easter. Then it's full speed ahead until summer vacation. All your teachers will tell you what they need to get done."

Great. Just like Mrs. Bosworth in sixth grade. She said school wasn't over 'till it was over. And, believe me, Mrs. Bosworth used every minute. My brain still hurt from the experience.

The hall was an interesting place during the change of classes. People jostled, waved, and yelled at each other. If I tried to understand even a single word people were saying, all I could hear was a constant hum, sort of like a swarm of bees.

"Colette." I thought I heard my name above the chatter but I needed to go all the way to the other side of the building. I didn't like being late so I just kept moving.

"Colette." I heard it again, this time louder. I turned around and there was Jake, waving. I stopped right in the middle of the hall and waited while people went around me.

"Your dad offered me a job. Thank you." His ever present smile stretched across his face.

"I didn't do anything," I said.

"You said I was a good worker."

"Oh, yeah. I did say that."

"Now I'll have some gas money for my car. Thanks again."

"Sure. I've got to go to class." At some point while I was talking to Jake, my face started feeling hot. I was red-faced, I was sure of it. I couldn't cover my face with my hands because I was holding my books and anyway, I didn't want my probably very red ears sticking out like a neon sign. "Bye," I said as I turned and sprinted toward the end of the hall.

It was my Saturday to work at our store. The store had originally been named Rossini's. After my dad became partners with Gramps, it changed to Rossini and McGiver. Now that my dad was the main pharmacist and Gramps was retired, Gramps thought the store should be just McGiver's.

"No way," my dad would say. "I like it just the way it is. It's where Gemma and I fell in love. At Rossini's." My mom and dad had both worked at the store when they were in high school.

"Think about it, John. It's your place now," Gramps said.

"No, Antonio. It will always be your place."

The store had two large rooms. The soda fountain had a semi circular counter with ten stools around it. If the stools were all taken, I was really busy. I made malts, sodas, sundaes, and scooped ice cream cones until my hands were frozen. Literally frozen. My dad wanted to put a couple of booths in the corner. I pictured myself running to get the order, running to make the order, and then running with the malt or soda back to the booth.

"Please don't," I said. "I just can't run that fast."

"I may have to hire someone else for the weekends anyway," my dad said. "We're busier and busier."

"Mom and I can usually handle it."

"I know. You do a great job. But you're not here every Saturday." Since my mom still worked at St. Anastasia's, a woman named Marie worked during the week. In the summer, Marie wanted to be home with her kids so my mom worked during the week and every Saturday.

"Are you going to hire somebody for the weekends I'm not there?"

"Marie said she'll work every other Saturday so that's okay for now. I can't be filling prescriptions and checking people out at the register at the same time." It was good that the store was busy because that meant my dad was managing the store okay without Gramps.

There were two large refrigerators and a low freezer in the same room as the soda fountain. We had milk, pop, and beer in bottles, popsicles, ice cream sandwiches, and frozen juice.

The second room had the pharmacy at one end, rows of shelves with supplies like diapers, band aids, aspirin, bandages, thermometers, candy, and the cash register. My dad wanted to add more shelves so that people could buy more when they were waiting for their prescriptions. As it was, when someone waited for a prescription they could get a free coke, phosphate, or any other soft drink at the soda fountain. It had been my Grandma Rose's idea during the Depression and we still used it. Most people waiting just ordered the free drink but sometimes they decided ice cream would be better.

"Hi, Colette." I heard Jake's familiar voice behind me.

"Hi, Jake. I didn't know you were working today." My dad told me the night before that Jake was coming in. I didn't dare touch the warmth rising from my neck to my face. I hoped my face wasn't red.

"Is your mom around?"

"She's in the back. I'll go get her." I hurried to the back room. "Mom, Jake's here."

"Okay, thanks." My mom didn't look up which I was thankful for because my face was burning. I decided to stop in the bathroom. I looked in the mirror and a blotchy red face looked back at me. I splashed cold water on my face and looked again. Better. Definitely better.

I walked out and Jake was still waiting by the register. "Mom will be right out. See you later." I went to the refrigerator by the soda fountain. I filled the canisters with toppings for sundaes and malts. There were separate containers for strawberries, pineapple, cherries, hot fudge, chocolate, butterscotch, and caramel.

My mom showed Jake the soda fountain, the pharmacy, and the shelves with all the supplies. They had to go to the back room where everything was kept in boxes. Jake would be responsible for keeping the shelves stocked. I was glad the day was busy with one customer after another. I didn't have time to think, believe me.

My mom and Jake stood by the counter. "So, we'll start with two days a week after school. Can you be here by three?"

"I have baseball practice every day after school," Jake said.

"That won't work, then." The store closed every day during the week at six o'clock and at five o'clock on Saturdays. "Okay, we'll have to stick with Saturdays for now. How about every Saturday?"

"I can do that."

"We'll make it ten to four then. See you next week."

"Thank you, Mrs. McGiver. See you next week."

So Jake was going to be working every Saturday. I'd have to see if I could work every Saturday too.

Chapter Twelve

Keep Your Eye on the Ball

Our first game started with all of us a little nervous. We didn't know how we were going to play. There was nothing worse than losing a game without even a chance of winning.

"What if I let the team down?" Suzy asked. She was almost panicky.

"Catcher is a very hard position. You're in the game with every pitch."

"Maybe I shouldn't be the catcher." Suzy kneaded her hands together.

"We're all in this together. I'm not perfect either."

"Okay, girls, gather round," Coach Richter said. "You all know what you're supposed to do. We worked on it at practice over and over. So, let's recap. You know where to throw the ball, when to steal second or third, how to keep your glove down on the ground, how to step into the ball when you swing, and how to swing level, not up at the ball. If you do all those things, we will have a good game. What's the one thing that we know for certain?"

"The game isn't over until the last out," several girls said in chorus.

"Good. You were listening during practice." Coach Richter took off his baseball cap and held it in his hands. "A quick prayer," he said. "Lord, this is our first game. Thank you for bringing us here today. Help us to play hard and at the same time show good sportsmanship. Amen."

Coach Richter talked about sportsmanship a lot; every single practice. He got mad if you got mad. I thought that was kind of funny. He would say that there was no place for anger during a softball game because it usually made you play in an inconsistent way. For instance, you might swing at a bad pitch and strike out. Or, you might throw the ball nowhere near the first baseman. He always gave us several examples like that. Then he would tell us that there were things absolutely prohibited on his team. No swearing for any reason and no yelling at a teammate. Cheering on a teammate was great and he wanted us to do that with enthusiasm.

"Go out there now and have fun," he said. "Positions. O'Malley – pitcher, Donohue – first, Zastrow – second, McGiver – third, Pearson – short, Flynn – left, Anderson – center, Schmit – right, and Malone – catcher. Let's go."

We were the home team so we ran out to our positions in the field. Suzy tried to put on her knee pads quickly. One of the girls helped her with the chest protector. She put on the face mask and crouched down behind the plate with her glove ready.

Behind home plate were a few stands for people to sit in. They were protected by a backstop between them and the catcher. I looked over and there were Aunt Florence, Gramps, and little Rosie. Gramps gave Rosie a ball glove for her first birthday. He held Rosie's glove up in the air for me to see.

The first batter was up. Sam wound up and threw the ball across the center of the plate. The batter watched it go by. "Strike," the umpire yelled. The batter dug in their shoes, swung the bat twice, and waited for the next pitch. The ball flew toward the plate and the batter swung too late. Suzy already had the ball in her glove. "Strike two." Sam wound up again and the ball sailed toward the plate. It really was a thing of beauty to watch her. The batter stuck her bat out and got a piece of the ball. It stopped about a foot in front of the plate. It was Suzy's ball but I didn't know if she realized that. There she was, pulling off her mask and grabbing the ball. She threw the ball perfectly to first base and the batter was out. Suzy looked over at me and smiled before she put her mask back on. Sam retired the side easily since the next two batters struck out. It was our turn to bat.

I was the lead batter. I got ready at the plate and swung the bat a couple of times while I stared down the pitcher. The first pitch flew by me. I didn't swing. "Strike," the umpire said. The next pitch came in right at the waist line. I swung and caught part of it. "Foul ball," the umpire yelled. I had two strikes on me and I didn't want to strike out. The third pitch came in a little lower but I swung anyway. I connected and the ball took off toward third base. I dropped the bat and dashed to first. I didn't slow down as I ran through the base. I was on base.

Coach Richter clapped his hands but didn't touch the side of his nose. I stayed on first, waiting for a hit or a signal from the coach. Donohue hit a pop up so she was an easy out. O'Malley was the third batter. For some reason she swung at the first pitch and a grounder snaked to second base. The second baseman threw the ball to the shortstop who touched second base and then rifled the ball to first. Double play. Our side was out.

The game was a real pitcher's duel. Both teams had base runners at times but neither of us scored through five innings. We only played seven innings so somebody had to hit the ball soon.

I had struck out my last time at the plate. It was my turn to hit again. I swung at the first pitch way too early. "Strike," the umpire yelled. I had to get my timing down. I didn't take my eye off the pitcher. Her arm went back and released the ball. I watched the ball coming in right above the waist. I stepped into it and swung as hard as I could. Crack. It was a line drive between short and third. I rounded first and ran toward second. I made it there, no problem. I hoped I would score because there wasn't much I liked better than running across home plate.

Donohue hadn't had a hit the whole game so she really wanted to get me home. She finally hit the ball after four fouls. It was a sizzling grounder that went past the second baseman into right field. I was off like a shot, hoping the coach would tell me to keep running. He waved me on toward home. I ran as fast as I could. People yelled from the stands and my whole team was standing up, screaming. I knew it was going to be close. The ball had been thrown to the second baseman from right field. The catcher waited right by the plate so they could tag me out. I had to turn it on. I put my head down a little and ran even faster. Aunt Florence yelled, "Go, Colette, go." My right foot touched the plate just as the ball landed in the catcher's mitt. She tagged me. The umpire yelled, "Safe, you're safe."

Our whole team cheered and patted me on the back. It was 1 to 0.

That was the only run we scored the whole game. The other team tied the score in the seventh inning with a solo homerun. The next batter was up. Crack. The ball smoked toward third. If it got by me, the ball was in left field. I kept my glove close to the ground. The ball slid into my glove and I hurled the ball to first base. One out. Two outs away from an extra inning.

The next two batters got on base. Sam was getting tired. There were runners on first and second. But not for long. They both took off for a double steal. Suzy threw the ball to second instead of third. Two outs, but there was a runner on third. Sam snapped her arm back and delivered a pitch into the dirt in front of the plate. It took a crazy hop and Suzy couldn't hang on to it. Suzy ran to the backstop to get the ball. The runner on third dashed toward home and scored before Suzy could throw the ball to Sam who was covering home plate. The game was over.

"When you're a catcher, you're supposed to catch the ball," Sam shrieked. She stood right in front of Suzy.

"I'm sorry," Suzy said. She looked down at the ground.

"You should be. You lost the game for us."

Sam had thrown her glove down and her fists were clenched. "You're so stupid," she said. "And really a bad catcher."

Suzy looked like she was ready to cry.

I said, "If you ask me, that was a wild pitch. A professional baseball player couldn't have caught it."

"Shut up, just shut up," Sam said. Her fists were still clenched and she was biting her bottom lip.

"There is no place for that on my team," Coach Richter said. "You threw a bad pitch. Let it go." Sam looked like she was going to say something and then changed her mind. The coach said if she ever did that again, she wouldn't be pitching the next game even if it was the last game of the season. "Part of playing sports is learning to lose," he said. "Graciously," he added. "We'll talk about this tomorrow at practice. Now go shake the other team's hands."

Chapter Thirteen

Keep the Change

It was my weekend to work again. I was more than looking forward to it because I'd be working with Jake all day. Gramps, my mom, and I were eating breakfast before Mom and I went to the store.

"Mom, do you like Jake?" I asked in a casual way. I took a bite of toast with homemade strawberry jam on it.

"I do and so does your dad."

"He sounds like he's a good addition," Gramps said.

"On the Saturday Colette doesn't work, he could be very valuable. We'll have Marie in the summer if we need her too."

"I told dad I can start working every Saturday. We don't have softball practice on Saturdays." I didn't say I really don't have enough to do since Sally and I don't have our all day talks anymore.

"You need one morning to sleep in, Colette. Jake can do the major stocking on the Saturday you work and then we might have other jobs for him on the other weekend."

My mom had finished her breakfast and was cleaning up. "Colette, are you coming with me this morning? I'm leaving in ten minutes." The store was about two miles from our house so my dad walked there on Saturdays. He liked to get everything ready before opening at ten o'clock.

"I can be ready."

I had been practicing conversations with the mirror so I could keep from blushing. I pretended that Jake said, "You look nice today, Colette." I responded with "Thanks." When I answered imaginary Jake with "So glad you noticed," my face turned red. So I went back to just plain "Thanks."

I looked at my thick, wild hair and there was nothing I could do to change that other than sleeping on rollers. I had brush rollers with picks that I had to stick through the roller into my head until the roller didn't move. I didn't sleep all night, believe me. Suzy told me she used orange juice cans with bobby pins and it worked great. Somehow she hooked the bobby pin onto a binder. She promised she would show me how to do it. For today, a pony tail was going to have to do.

Jake walked in right at ten o'clock. He wrote his time down on his time card. "Hi, Colette. How's softball going?" He asked.

"Great. Your sister's a great pitcher." I guess I was going to answer great to everything he said.

"She is. She practices in our back yard all the time. We have a home plate set up. Sometimes I use it too."

I tell you, I could have listened to him all day. I had lots and lots of questions. Did you always pitch? Does your arm get sore? What do you do then? What's your best pitch? How do you throw a curve ball? Instead of asking him any questions, I said, "That's so cool."

"Jake, let's start in the back," my mom said. She turned to me. "Colette, you may have to handle the soda fountain and the register until I come back."

"Sure, no problem." I looked around. There was no one in the store so at least for now it was no problem. Usually, I worked in the soda fountain while my mom was at the register. In a pinch I could ring the register but there were certain items like cigarettes I was not supposed to ring up.

I was still waiting for a customer when my mom and Jake came out of the backroom. He had a pad with him and a pencil. They went over to the shelves and he wrote down what was needed. Then they went to the backroom to find the merchandise. I was happy to see customers because I liked to be busy at work and it kept me from staring at Jake. I went back and forth from the soda fountain to the cash register.

At four o'clock, Jake stopped at the register. He had a pack of cigarettes in his hand. He put two quarters on the counter. He wasn't eighteen and I wasn't supposed to check out cigarettes. I looked around for my mom or dad.

"Something wrong, Sport?"

"Well, I'm not supposed to..."

"To what?"

"My dad said I can't..."

Jake stood there with his arms crossed and his eyebrows raised. I was getting so flustered at this point; I didn't know what to say. My mom was busy and so was my dad. "Never mind," I said. "Are you buying this?"

"That's what it looks like." He flashed his grin and I thought, what's the harm?

"Okay. That's forty cents."

"Keep the change, Sport." He winked.

I rang them up under miscellaneous. All of a sudden I remembered Musolf's store. I wondered if he had a pack in his pocket. No, he wouldn't do that. I put both quarters in the till and closed it. I stood there for a minute. I reopened the till, reached into my pocket where I kept my tips, and put another thirty cents in the till.

My mom came over. "It was a good day today. I'm so glad you talked to your dad about Jake."

"Sure, Mom." I didn't recognize it at the time but I felt funny. Not ha, ha funny but kind of unsettled. Yeah, that was it; unsettled. I couldn't wait to get home.

Chapter Fourteen

Babysitting is Great

Aunt Florence wanted me to babysit on Saturday. I was still boycotting her because of how much she paid me but she begged me. And I mean BEGGED me. She and Mike needed a date and she had been working so much and Rosie loved me so much and... Really, it was a full frontal assault. I finally said yes. Actually, I said, "I suppose I could."

"Great," Aunt Florence said. "I'll tell Mike." She hugged me. "Thank you, Colette."

I was so tired after working at the store that I wished I had held out and said no. Uncle Mike and Aunt Florence had reservations at the St. James Hotel for six o'clock. I barely had time to get home, say hi to Gramps, have dinner, and get to Aunt Florence's by ten to six.

Rosie jumped up and down when she saw me. Well, it wasn't exactly jumping because she would have fallen down. It was more like she shifted her position from foot to foot really fast. I couldn't resist little Rosie any more than Gramps could so in no time I was holding her. Aunt Florence and Uncle Mike left saying they wouldn't be late. Rosie could go to bed about seven thirty or eight o'clock.

I thought it would be a good idea to walk up to the park. It was only two blocks away. "C'mon, Rosie. Want to go to the park?" I pushed her stroller on the sidewalk. It was seventy five degrees and sunny without a cloud in the sky. A perfect May day in Minnesota. I guess it wasn't so bad babysitting after all.

"Hi, Sport." Jake was coming out of his house. "Wow, I just said goodbye to you a little while ago. Are you sure you aren't following me?" He smiled and winked like he had when I rang up his cigarettes.

"No. I'm not following you." I felt my face get hot. "I'm babysitting my cousin."

"I can see that. I'm just kidding."

"My aunt lives on the next block. I didn't even know you lived here."

"Relax, Sport, I was kidding."

I didn't like him calling me Sport. It sounded like I was in grade school.

"Gotta go," he said.

I didn't even say goodbye. He thought I was following him. I was so embarrassed. Rosie sat on the swing while I pushed her. My spirits lifted a little because every time she went up in the air, she said, "Whee" in her high-pitched voice.

I took a different route going back to Aunt Florence's so I wouldn't have to walk by Jake's. Rosie and I looked at books after she got her pajamas on. She pointed to all the animals in the books and I had to make the sounds. "Roar." "Moo." "Baa." I put her in bed at eight o'clock.

I didn't feel so tired anymore. I got a bowl of potato chips and went into the living room to turn on the TV. The house had a large front window. It was a good vantage point to watch neighbors so Aunt Florence seemed to know everything that was going on across the street and in the neighborhood in general. I looked out and saw Jake's blue Fairlane racing up and down the street. He wasn't alone; in fact, his car was full of kids. They whooped out the window.

I couldn't tell who was with him but I didn't want him to see me. I ducked down. I heard shouting and I had to look out. Neighbors had opened their doors and were yelling, "Slow down." Jake blasted his horn and he was on his way.

Aunt Florence and Uncle Mike were home by nine o'clock. I told them all about Rosie swinging at the park. They wanted to know everything we did together, if she said anything besides "Hi," if she went to bed okay, and what books we read. All the while they looked at each other and beamed. Aunt Florence had these really cool blue-gray eyes with golden flecks in the middle. When she was happy or excited about something, the flecks took on a life of their own and danced around. As I talked about little Rosie, the golden flecks flew around her eyes and sparkled.

"Anything else happen?" Aunt Florence asked.

"No, nothing else." I didn't tell her about Jake speeding up and down the street because really nothing had happened.

"Good," she said. Aunt Florence started to reach into her purse.

Here comes the dollar, I thought.

Uncle Mike stopped her. "Remember what we talked about, Florence?"

"I remember."

He turned toward me. "We decided that you should get a raise for your babysitting. We couldn't find another babysitter who loves Rosie like you do. What do you think about seventy five cents an hour?"

"I think that's great," I said. I made a dollar twenty five cents an hour at the store plus tips but this was different. Seventy five cents was generous for babysitting.

"So, we were gone for a little over three hours. Is two dollars fifty cents fair?"

I was expecting a dollar from Aunt Florence so it was more than fair. "It's fair. Thank you." Half my salary from the store went into savings. Now adding the two fifty to the money I made at the store that day made me very happy. I'd have to look at my stash of money at home and maybe I had enough to buy a new pair of bellbottom jeans.

Uncle Mike drove me home. Gramps and my mom and dad were watching the Carol Burnett show, which we all liked. I sat down with them. At the commercial, my mom asked how the babysitting went.

"Great," I said.

"Oh really. I thought you didn't like babysitting."

"Uncle Mike said they'd be paying me seventy five cents an hour now. I got two fifty. So it was great."

"Isn't that interesting?" My mom said.

I looked at her and wondered if she had something to do with my raise. She would never tell me she had talked to Aunt Florence about paying me a dollar but I bet she did.

"Oh, Carol Burnett's back on now. Shh," she said.

Chapter Fifteen

Prom

The juniors and seniors had been getting ready for the prom for weeks. In fact, that's all they talked about. The school was literally abuzz with prom talk. The dance was held in the gym so it would be closed for classes from Wednesday on. There was a committee set up to decorate the whole gym and the stage where the live band would play. It was coming up this weekend, the second weekend in May.

Freshmen couldn't go to the prom and sophomores had to be asked by a junior or senior so I was out of luck. Not that I wanted to go myself but it would be fun to see the girls in their gowns and the boys in their tuxes. I asked Suzy if she was interested and she said, "It would be fun to see everyone dressed up."

We put our names in as people who would like to help but the teachers in charge told us they had enough helpers. Suzy didn't seem to care as much as I did. I really wanted to see Jake in a tuxedo. He told me his old girlfriend asked him and he couldn't say no.

In homeroom, Sally and Sam had their heads together, smiling and laughing. I had just heard that Suzy and I couldn't help so I wondered what was so funny. I didn't have to wonder for long because they started talking so loud; I swear they could have been heard in another building.

"Isn't that great?" Sally said. She slapped Sam on the shoulder.

"It's great. I guess I'm surprised though," Sam said.

"Why? We put our names in a long time ago."

"So did other people and they were turned down."

"Maybe they thought since our brothers are going to the prom, we would be the best helpers." She crossed her arms across her chest and sighed.

The whole class stared as they bragged and bragged. I had to look away.

"Girls, quiet down," Mrs. Crenshaw said. "Take your seats. Hurry up. I have a few announcements."

Everybody sat down.

Mrs. Crenshaw continued. "The gym is closed Wednesday, Thursday, and Friday. All of you will miss either one or two gym classes. We have several choices of things you can do during your gym time. I'll put the signup sheet on the board. Please look at it today and decide what you want to do."

I wanted to make sure I wasn't stuck with a teacher I didn't like or with Sally and Sam. Suzy was in my gym class on Wednesday and Friday. I thought I should check the options before I changed class. "Suzy, what do you want to do?"

"I don't know," she said. "Let's look."

The names of all the freshmen teachers were on top of the sheets. There were also several lines on each sheet for the student's names. Most of the teachers wanted help with correcting papers. Mrs. Crenshaw wanted people going through books and erasing any pencil marks in them. Suzy and I signed up for one day of that and one day in the library filing books.

I always sat next to Suzy at lunch now. I couldn't believe how obnoxious Sam and Sally were as they carried on about their treasured positions checking coats at the prom. Maybe no one would be wearing coats if the weather was warm enough. So Sally and Sam would be standing all by themselves with nothing to do. It was a pleasant thought.

I wasn't working on the day of the prom so I needed something to do. "Suzy, what are you doing on Saturday?"

"I don't have any plans."

"Do you want to get together?"

"What do you have in mind?"

"I don't know. But I don't want to be home all day and all night."

"Me either. Maybe you can come over. I'll check with my mom."

On Saturday, my mom dropped me off at Suzy's house at seven o'clock. Suzy introduced me to her mom and dad, and her two younger brothers, Matt and Jim. "Suzy said you've really helped her with softball," Mrs. Malone said.

"She's gotten a lot better because she works hard at it," I said.

"And you helped me," Suzy said. "Want to go to my room?"

We walked down to the end of the hall. "I'm glad I'm the only girl because I get a room to myself," she said. Suzy's brothers were nine and eleven and they shared a room.

She had a double bed, a dresser, a bedside stand with a lamp, a small chair, and shelves filled with books on one wall. "Have you read all of these?" I asked.

"Yep."

"Could I borrow some now that summer's almost here?"

"Sure. Why don't you sit in the chair? I'll sit on the bed."

We talked about the prom and what people would be wearing. Suzy said, "Maybe we'll go next year."

I told her about getting all dressed up for Aunt Florence's wedding. And having my hair put on top of my head. "I had so much hairspray in my hair," I said. "It was impossible to brush it out the next day. It took me two hours."

"Wow. I suppose all the girls going to prom had their hair done."

"Good luck tomorrow is all I have to say."

"Colette, I'm going to ask you something."

"Okay."

"You don't have to answer if you don't want to."

"Okay."

"What happened between you and Sally? I mean, the two of you were always together."

"It's a long story." I thought, what have I got to lose. "If I tell you this, you have to promise not to tell anyone. And I mean anyone."

"I promise."

I told her about Sally thinking she had a date with Jake, Jake sitting with me because the theater was full, and then Sally blaming me for the whole fiasco.

"Wow. Why won't she talk to you about it?"

"She's a proud person. I didn't think it was a date from the beginning and I told her that. Anyway, that's what happened."

"I wonder what Sally and Sam are doing right now."

We were back to talking about the prom. Mrs. Malone took me home at ten o'clock. "See you Monday," I said before I left the car.

Even though we had heard about the prom for weeks before the event, the whole week after that's all anyone talked about at school. I got to the point where I just didn't want to hear another word about dresses, hair styles, shoes, the dance, the band, or the after parties. Anyone who had a brother or sister who went to the prom talked about it non-stop. Of course, Sally and Sam acted like they had been invited by the royal family and they were the princesses.

The good thing was a whole year had to pass before the school buzzed with prom talk again.

Chapter Sixteen
Our Little Secret

Our softball team was doing really well. Sam was truly a fantastic pitcher and Suzy had settled into the catching spot like it was made for her. Coach Richter started each practice with "I'm a happy man. Happy to coach such a hard-working group of girls."

We had two games left in the regular season. If we won both of them, we went to the championship game in Lake City. Lake City was a town south of Red Wing and on the Mississippi. This part of the Mississippi River was called Lake Pepin because the river was so wide that it actually looked like a lake. Water skiing started on Lake Pepin; at least that was the claim. I think it was right because people sure loved to water ski on Lake Pepin. On windy days, hundreds of sailboats dotted the lake.

My favorite thing of all was eagles circling as they soared over the water. If I was really lucky, I might see one of them swoop toward the water. I had never seen an eagle grasp a fish in its talons but I always hoped I would. Gramps said it was one of his favorite things in the world.

The next weekend I worked, I wasn't quite so anxious to see Jake. I didn't want to be checking out his cigarettes at the end of the day while he winked at me.

He seemed to be busy enough walking back and forth to stock the shelves. He told my dad that he could deliver prescriptions too. Sometimes a person couldn't get to the store and then my dad had to close the pharmacy or deliver the prescription after the store closed.

"Thanks, Jake. I may have you do that," my dad said. "That's right. You have your own car."

"Yes, sir," he said.

The soda fountain was busy since it was warm outside and everyone was thinking about ice cream.

Jake came over a couple of times to see how I was doing. I said, "I'm busy." I couldn't believe I just wanted him to leave me alone.

In the afternoon, Jake's friends came into the store. Sally's brother, John, Mike, and some other guy who I didn't know were all talking to Jake. I couldn't take my eyes off them. If they started walking down the aisles, I'd be walking right next to them, believe me.

"Colette, are you okay?" My mother stood by the counter of the soda fountain.

"Sure, Mom. Why do you ask?"

"Because you have customers."

There were two people sitting at the counter I hadn't even noticed. "Sorry," I said. "Mom, can we switch now? My hands are really cold." I rubbed my hands together.

"Okay. You take the register then."

I took off my apron and walked over to the register. No one was waiting. Good. I walked to the aisle where Jake and his friends were. I stood there with my arms crossed.

They stopped talking. I didn't move. "Sport, is something wrong?" Jake asked.

"No, there's nothing wrong. I'm keeping an eye on all of you. I want you to know that." My heart pounded in my chest.

"Why?" Jake asked. His eyes were narrowed and I couldn't tell what his half-smile meant other than he was mad.

"You know why. If I have to ask you to empty your pockets, I will." I looked around at all of them.

"We better go," John said.

I started to walk away and thought of something else. I turned around and looked Jake right in the eye. "Stop calling me Sport. I don't like it."

From the register, I could see that Jake's friends were all leaving. I took in a deep breath. Maybe I should tell my parents about Musolf's store and what happened there. Of course, now they both loved Jake. I would have to explain that the reason I wanted him working at our store was to get back at Sally. And I'd have to explain that I actually ate the candy bar that was in my pocket, knowing that it was stolen. I should have told Tommy Musolf. Anyway, stealing was not going to happen in our store. Not if I could help it.

Jake didn't come to the register with cigarettes for me to ring up. Maybe he had gotten the message.

Aunt Florence had asked me to babysit early in the week. I said yes right away. I was really close to having enough money for the jeans I wanted.

Aunt Florence and Uncle Mike said they'd be gone about three hours again. I couldn't decide if I should take Rosie to the park because I didn't want to walk past Jake's house. I could take a different route. It would take longer but Rosie liked riding in the stroller so that's what I decided to do.

I put Rosie in the stroller in front of the house. I was just starting to push her when I saw Jake's Ford Fairlane coming down the street. I couldn't hide so I just stood there hoping he wouldn't see me. The car went roaring by and then stopped in the middle of the street.

Jake rolled down the window. "I didn't want to drive by without saying hi," he said.

"Hi," I said.

He drove away. I didn't have to take my alternative route so I walked right by Jake's house. Sam and Sally were sitting on the front steps. Great. I didn't know what to do so I waved. Sam waved back and I thought I saw a little wave from Sally. Maybe she was starting to thaw. I wondered if she missed our conversations as much as I did.

Rosie and I spent an hour at the park. I pushed her home in the stroller and got her ready for bed. We sat down with our pile of books. Really, there was something so sweet about her when she sat on my lap while I read to her. At eight o'clock, I put Rosie into her crib. She gave me a big hug before she lay down. Maybe I would babysit more often.

I planned to watch TV until Aunt Florence and Uncle Mike got home. I went out to the kitchen to get some root beer and potato chips. The front door bell rang. Who could that be? I looked out the front window. Jake and Mike were standing there.

I opened the front door. "What are you doing here?"

"We came to say hi. Aren't you going to let us in?" Jake said. They had opened the screen door.

"No, you can't come in." I stood in front of them.

"I thought we were friends, Colette." Jake smiled his great smile.

At least he didn't call me Sport. "I guess we're friends," I said.

"Good. I thought so." Jake came into the living room and I moved out of the way because I didn't want to push him. Jake and Mike looked around. I felt uncomfortable because

Sally was the only person who had ever come babysitting with me.

"I 'm not supposed to have people over when I..." I said.

Jake interrupted me with, "I won't tell if you won't."

"What exactly do you want?"

"Nothing." He motioned to Mike and the two of them sat down.

I thought, then why are you here? I didn't sit down. I had nothing to say to either of them. "Aunt Florence will be back soon. In fact, they're on their way right now." I crossed my arms.

"Okay, I get the idea. You don't want your aunt coming home and finding us here."

"Right."

The inside screen door was still open. Jake and Mike started walking toward it. Jake stopped and turned around. "By the way, where's the liquor cabinet?"

"I don't know," I said.

"Let's see, it's usually in the dining room." Jake walked into the dining room. "Here it is, just like I said." He opened the cabinet and pulled out a bottle. "Whiskey. Good," he said.

"What are you doing?" I said. I wanted to yell but I knew I'd wake up Rosie. "Get out."

"Mike, go get me some water, will you?" Mike hadn't moved from the living room. He did now. People tended to obey Jake.

"I said get out," I said.

"We will in a minute, Sport. Don't worry." Jake looked into the kitchen. "Mike, that jar by the sink will be perfect. Bring a glass of water too." Aunt Florence made jams and jellies so she always had jars in the kitchen.

I tell you, my face was burning. It wasn't from embarrassment. I was mad, really mad.

Mike went out to the kitchen and came back with an empty jar and a glass full of water. Jake grabbed the jar, poured some of the whiskey into it, and then screwed on the cover. Then he poured the water into the bottle until it was at the exact place that it had been with the whiskey in it. "Perfect," he said.

I stared at both of them in disbelief. "It isn't perfect," I yelled. "I told you to get out," I yelled even louder. I heard crying but it didn't register for a minute. "I'm going to tell my aunt you did this," I screamed.

"I don't think you will," Jake said. "It's our little secret." He held his finger up to his mouth.

Rosie was crying really hard by this time. I had to go get her. Jake and Mike walked out the door. I think Jake said thanks, Sport, before I slammed the door.

Rosie stood in her crib with tears running down her face. She put her arms up for me and I picked her up. "Shh, it's okay. We'll go look at books again until your mom and dad get home."

I had to check to make sure the whiskey was put away. It was back in the cabinet already and the glass of water was by the sink. I put Rosie down on the floor and she started crying again. I rinsed out the glass and put it upside down in the drying rack. "Rosie, hang on," I said. They had taken a jar so I had to put another one by the sink. Aunt Florence had all her jars in the pantry next to her wonderful jams. I didn't know if the jar had been upside down with a cover on top but that's what I did. It was going to have to do.

I picked up Rosie and brought her back to the living room. We looked at all her favorite books. I wrapped her blanket around her and pretty soon she had calmed down.

She was still sucking her thumb when Aunt Florence and Uncle Mike came home.

"What happened?" Uncle Mike asked. He picked Rosie up. "Were you crying?"

"She was," I said.

"Why?" Aunt Florence asked.

I should have told her why. That Jake and his weird buddy, Mike, came into the house, sat in the living room even though I told them to leave, and then stole some of Uncle Mike's whiskey. Instead I just sat there and said, "I don't know. I thought maybe she had a bad dream."

"Maybe. Oh, poor little Rosie." Aunt Florence took Rosie from Uncle Mike.

I hadn't noticed the dirt on the floor earlier. Jake and Mike must have had dirt on their shoes when they came in. There was some on the floor in front of the liquor cabinet. Uncle Mike saw me looking at the dirt. He went into the dining room and stood by the liquor cabinet. He opened the door of the cabinet and closed it. He walked into the kitchen. He came back into the living room, rubbing his chin. "Was someone here?"

"Uh. No," I said.

"Where did the dirt come from?"

"I don't know." I didn't dare breathe. Uncle Mike was one of my favorite people and now he was locking his eyes with mine. I had to look away. "C'mon, Colette. I'll take you home."

I wanted to get out of there. Uncle Mike was usually talkative when he drove me home. We sat in the car saying nothing until we got to my house. "Are you sure nothing happened?" Uncle Mike asked.

He knew something was wrong. Jake was right. I wasn't going to tell on him. "No, not that I know of."

"Okay. We'll see you later then."

I couldn't get out of the car fast enough and evidently Uncle Mike felt that way too because he sped off as soon as I opened the door of my house. My mom looked up from the couch. "Good," she said. "Carol Burnett is just starting."

"I think I'm going to bed, Mom."

"How was babysitting?"

"Fine. It was fine."

"Okay. You've had a long day. See you tomorrow."

I trudged upstairs. I didn't know what Uncle Mike was thinking but he wasn't buying the bad dream story. He was probably talking to Aunt Florence right now.

One thing was certain. Jake was a jerk; a total jerk. The farther I stayed away from him the better.

Chapter Seventeen
Bad News Travels Fast

The next morning was Sunday so we went to nine o'clock Mass. I sat next to Gramps. He said the prayers, sang along with the choir, and patted my knee about ten times during Mass. We went out to breakfast at the Diner. I kept thinking about Jake taking the whiskey. I wondered if Uncle Mike would figure out that it had been tampered with.

"Your softball team is doing well," my dad said.

"It is," I said.

"Do you think you'll go to Lake City?"

"Maybe."

"I mean for the championship," my dad said.

"I know."

"Are you okay?"

"I'm okay, Dad. I just don't have a lot to say today."

"Sometimes a girl needs to think," Gramps said. He took a big bite of his pancakes smothered with butter and syrup.

"That's right, Gramps," I said. I could usually count on Gramps being on my side. The way he said that I needed to think could mean a couple of things. That I just wanted quiet; unlikely because I loved to talk about everything or he knew something was bothering me big time. That was probably the case but I wasn't going to say anything because then I would have to tell him what was bothering me.

Ever since my fight with Sally, Gramps had tried to get me to talk to him. So had my mom. I couldn't tell them how I had been part of a big lie to Mrs. Reynolds. I couldn't tell them that I knew about stealing from Musolf's and I had said nothing even though Mr. Musolf was Gramp's best friend. I really couldn't tell them about Uncle Mike's whiskey being watered down because Aunt Florence and Uncle Mike wouldn't want me babysitting anymore. I should have kept Jake from coming into their house.

My mom said that good news traveled fast in our town but bad news traveled like a lightning bolt. I didn't have to wonder about the bad news part because the phone was ringing as we walked into the house. It was Aunt Florence.

My mom kept saying "I see" and "No, she didn't say anything" while looking at me. I went upstairs, put a Chicago album on my record player, and lay on the bed. I had a sick feeling that the phone call had something to do with last night.

"Colette, come downstairs, will you?" My mom yelled.

"Colette," my dad yelled. This was going downhill fast. I sat on the edge of the bed, wondering what to do. I didn't wonder for long. I heard a knock at my door a second before my dad opened it. "Please turn off your music and come downstairs," my dad said quietly. "We have some questions for you."

"I'll be right there." I took the needle off the record, shut off the record player, put my record in its jacket, and then laid it on the shelf underneath. My dad didn't move. He waited until I crossed in front of him and then he followed me.

My mom sat in the living room. Gramps was nowhere to be seen. "Sit down," my mom said. She motioned to the big chair that Gramps usually sat in. My mom and dad sat down on the couch. "Florence had some interesting things to say about last night," my mom said.

I swallowed. "Really?"

"Yes, really."

"What did she say?"

"We'll get to that in a minute. Why don't you tell me what happened last night?"

"I don't know what you mean."

My dad held his hand up. "Let me try, Gemma," he said. "Honey, we're your parents and we only want the best for you." He had his hands on his lap. His voice was quiet. I leaned forward so I didn't miss a word. "Mike noticed dirt on the floor; some was in front of his liquor cabinet. His whiskey bottle was in a different spot and the cap was loose. He tasted it and he said it was watered down. Do you know anything about that?"

"No. No, I don't." I looked down at the floor. I had never lied to my parents or Gramps. How did Jake know that I would lie for him?

"Well, we're not getting the truth obviously," my dad said. He stood up and paced. "Let's try again. Mike said the whiskey was watered down. You were the only one there. Or were you?" My dad stopped in front of my chair.

I squirmed. "I was."

"What happened to the whiskey?"

I thought I might as well get it over with. "I took it," I said.

"Why?"

"I don't know why."

"Where did you get the idea?"

"Kids at school. Some said that they took liquor from their parents, added water to it, and their parents had no idea. So that's why I did it."

"Just because kids at school were doing it?"

"Yes, that's why."

"I never thought of you as being a follower. We'll have to keep a much closer eye on you," my mom said. She stood next to my dad; a real united front. "We'll tell you your punishment later. In fact, you can go."

"Where's the whiskey now?" My dad asked.

"What do you mean?" I squirmed again.

"I mean, what did you do with it? Did you drink it?"

"No." I was starting to panic. I was afraid I'd tell the whole story. Then my babysitting career would be done forever. And worse than that, people at school would call me a tattletale. "Actually, I took a taste of it and I didn't like it. Not one bit. So I dumped it out." My head was aching. "Can I go?" I asked.

"Go ahead," my mom said. "I'm not going to tell you how disappointed we are or how once you lose trust in somebody, it's hard to get it back. We'll talk about that later. By the way, Florence, Mike, and Rosie are coming for dinner."

Great. I'll have two more people staring at me and asking me questions. Maybe I should just sit in the middle of the table with the rump roast or whatever we were having. Then everyone could gape at me while Aunt Florence said, "Tsk, tsk."

This was becoming one of the worst weekends of my life. The very worst in my life was after Gramps had a stroke and we thought we were going to lose him. It was horrible being in the hospital and not knowing what was going to happen. Another one was when Sally decided that I was the reason why Jake wasn't her date. I didn't know if we would ever be able to fix it because she hadn't talked to me in two months. I'd like to tell her that she was lucky she wasn't Jake's date because she'd be in as much trouble as me.

My body felt heavy like something was pushing me down. I had nobody I could talk to about it. Sally was out as a confidant and Suzy was really nice but she didn't really know my family. She didn't know about Aunt Florence and her son, Daniel, who was twenty one years old. And she didn't know about my Uncle Daniel, who had died in the Korean War. She didn't know how much I loved my Gramps, how I had the coolest dad ever, and how my mom had never lied to me about anything.

Chapter Eighteen
Consequences

I lay down on my bed and went to sleep. There was knocking at the door, right before it was opened.

"Colette. Wake up," my dad said. "It's three in the afternoon."

My mom was standing there too. I sat up on the bed.

"We might as well get right to it." My dad was very serious. "Your mother and I are in agreement that there has to be some consequences. I mean, I know that kids drink and party and do all kinds of things."

I just sat there. I didn't know if I should agree or disagree or respond at all.

"You're only fourteen and a half and because of that, we have to be sure this doesn't happen again. You've got three years left in high school. So..."

I had never been grounded. I wondered how long it was going to be.

"You're grounded for three weeks. This is how we came up with it. I said a month because of the fact that you stole from your uncle in such a sneaky way." He ran his fingers through his wavy brown hair. "Your mother said two weeks so we compromised."

THREE WEEKS. That's a little excessive, I should say. My dad was rambling on and on. I didn't even hear him anymore.

"I said do you have any questions?" My dad asked.

"What about softball?"

"I'm sorry, you're grounded."

"What? I can't play!" I was standing now. "That's not fair." I looked over at my mom. "Mom, do you agree that I can't play?"

"Talk to your father. I'm sorry."

"I think I'll just stay up here. I'm not hungry anyway." I had to think about this whole big mess. Maybe I'd tell them that I didn't want to work at the store anymore. "Please go," I said.

My mom started saying something and then closed her mouth. They both walked out of the room. I didn't exactly slam the door but I closed it with a bang. I went over to my records and looked at them. I put three Beatle's records on the spindle and one of them dropped onto the turntable. I turned it up loud, really loud. Usually that would bring a knock on the door from my mom but nothing happened so I turned it up louder. No knock. Good. I sang along.

I still didn't know if I was going to sit at the dining room table with Uncle Mike and Aunt Florence. On the other hand, I couldn't just sit up in my room for three weeks. THREE WEEKS. I almost wished that I had done something so the punishment didn't seem so unfair.

The second record was just about done when I heard a knock at the door. "What?" I shouted. The door opened. I expected my mom but instead it was Aunt Florence holding Rosie. Rosie held her hands over her ears. I turned off the music.

"Rosie was looking for you, Colette," Aunt Florence said.

"I thought you wouldn't want to see me."

"Well, I'm glad you said what happened."

"Yes."

Rosie reached for me and I took her. I gave her a hug. She put her head on my shoulder.

"Where did you dump the whiskey?" Aunt Florence asked. "I mean after you had a sip."

"Um. In the backyard."

"Our backyard?"

"Oh, yeah. Your backyard."

Aunt Florence seemed puzzled. Then she smiled. "Maybe I should ask Mike to go sniff around in the backyard."

"Are you mad at me?"

"No, I'm not mad because I don't think you drank some whiskey and threw the rest in our backyard. Oh, and then you filled the bottle with water. That about right?"

"I guess so."

"Okay, Colette. You can talk to me when you're ready to."

On the one hand, I was glad that Aunt Florence didn't believe that I stole Uncle Mike's whiskey but I had been punished and that wasn't going to change.

"Are you coming downstairs?" Aunt Florence took Rosie from me.

"In a few minutes." I didn't quite know how to take all of Aunt Florence's questions. Why did she call my mom and get her all upset? Now, she basically told me she knew I didn't do anything. It was confusing. Everybody was telling me to talk to them. I needed Sally to figure it all out.

That night my mom made fried chicken and mashed potatoes. She also made chicken gravy that was out of this world so even though I didn't have a big appetite, I couldn't pass up the whole meal. And if Aunt Florence made one of her famous pies, I guess I was going to have a piece of that too.

When I walked downstairs I thought everyone would be staring at me. Rosie was sitting on Gramp's lap. He looked up for a second and had Rosie wave to me. Maybe he wasn't mad at me. Actually I couldn't think of a time when Gramps was mad at me. So, Gramps and Aunt Florence were on my side, maybe. I had to figure out how I could still play softball. The grounding was so unfair, I couldn't believe it.

Uncle Mike and my dad were sitting with Gramps and Rosie so Aunt Florence and my mom must be in the kitchen.

Uncle Mike and my dad didn't even look up so they were mad. Okay, two against two. My mom was the tie-breaker. Aunt Florence already told me that she knew I hadn't taken Uncle Mike's whiskey. Maybe she was talking to my mom right now about it. I thought maybe I should stay out of the kitchen. The problem was I knew what had happened last night and I had lied about it.

Well, I only had the choice of the kitchen or the living room so the kitchen was it. At least, I could help bring the food to the table and it gave me something to do. I walked into the kitchen and the conversation stopped dead. I guess they had been talking about me.

"Can I help with anything?" I said.

"No, I think we're fine," my mom said.

My mom obviously wanted to get back to the conversation without me around. I started walking out of the kitchen. Upstairs was the place for me. I'd listen to music until dinner was on the table.

"I need some help with the dinner rolls," Aunt Florence said. "Colette, will you take them out of the bag and put them in a basket. You know the routine."

My mom put the rolls in a paper bag sprinkled with a fair amount of water and then put them in the oven to warm up. I got a hot pad because the bag was really hot and put them in a basket lined with a linen napkin. I put another linen napkin over them to keep them warm. I took them to the table with a stick of butter on a plate.

I took my time going back into the kitchen. The mashed potatoes were ready with circles of melted butter on the top and a little paprika. There was corn in another bowl. I grabbed both bowls and brought them to the table. Usually Gramps was sitting at his place from the minute the rolls arrived but he was far too busy in the living room making Rosie laugh.

I decided to sit down and wait for the rest of the family. My mom and Aunt Florence brought a huge platter of fried chicken to the table. It smelled delicious.

"C'mon, everybody. Dinner's ready," my mom said.

Rosie sat in the high chair. Uncle Mike and Aunt Florence were on either side of her. She was the main attraction so I didn't need to talk at all. My subjects were limited anyway. I couldn't talk about softball since I was banned from it for three weeks. I couldn't talk about Sally and the Reynolds family, a great conversation subject, because I hadn't been over there for two months. I couldn't talk about the store because Jake would come into the conversation.

I chose not to look at Uncle Mike and my dad who were busy chatting away about the Minnesota Twins baseball team and how their season was going. Gramps waved and clapped for Rosie. Aunt Florence and my mom were talking about her retirement from St. Anastasia's School.

"Eat up, everybody," my mom said. "Don't forget, Florence made a lemon meringue pie. Does anybody want anything? Cup of coffee?"

"I'll have a cup," Gramps said.

"Me too," said Aunt Florence.

"John, coffee?" my mom asked.

"No thanks, Gemma."

Uncle Mike hadn't said a word to me the whole dinner. Now he mumbled something.

"I'll take that as a yes for coffee," my mom said. My mom brought people their coffee and Aunt Florence followed with her pie.

"Delicious pie, Aunt Florence. May I have another piece," I said.

"Me too," Gramps said.

"Help yourself." Aunt Florence looked at me and smiled.

I had two friends in the family; Aunt Florence and Gramps. Since both of them loved my softball games, maybe I could get them to help change my punishment. At least, the no softball part of it.

Chapter Nineteen

Too Many Cooks

I told Suzy at lunch that I was grounded for three weeks. Suzy was very upset when she found out that I wouldn't be going to practice or the games either for the whole three weeks.

"What if we're in the championship? I can't even think about the championship without you at third."

"Talk to my mom and dad about it," I said.

"I wonder what Coach Richter is going to say," Suzy said.

"My mom said she'd call him today."

"What did you do? I was grounded for one weekend once and I thought that was bad."

Suzy knew Jake was working at our store but she didn't know I had recommended him for all the wrong reasons.

She didn't know about Musolf's either and I wasn't going to tell her about my babysitting disaster. I knew she wouldn't tell anybody if I confided in her but I wasn't ready to do that. "I can't talk about it."

"Did you lie? That's something that drives my parents crazy. In fact, that's why I was grounded. I lied about where I was going because I wanted to go somewhere else. My mom went into a long speech about how once trust is lost, it's hard to get it back."

"My mom says that too."

"So you did lie. Well, it must have been a doozy."

It was a funny thing now because I wasn't one bit interested in catching Jake's eye in the hall or hoping he would smile at me. The good thing about that was I wouldn't be red-faced anymore when I was talking to him. I didn't want to be working with him at all.

"When I was grounded, I was with my parents all the time. I didn't go off to my room. I hoped they'd get sick of me." Suzy took a big bite of her ham sandwich.

"You're a genius. I'm going to be with my mom so much, she's going to want to get away from me."

"You'll have to tell me how it works out."

To tell you the truth, I couldn't wait to get home. Instead of lying on my bed, listening to Blood, Sweat, and Tears or Chicago while I felt sorry for myself, I went into the kitchen to help my mom.

She was surprised to say the least. She kept saying things like, "Don't you have any homework?" and "You don't need to be helping." Then she said, "I'm surprised you're not listening to music."

I said, "Oh, no. I want to learn all about cooking. After all, I'm going to have to cook someday. You know, when I have a family."

My mom raised her eyebrows. She said, "But..." and then closed her mouth.

Good. She was getting nervous. "What did you say, Mom?" I had the potato peeler in my hand. I went to the sink to wash the five large potatoes she had out.

"Nothing. I didn't say anything."

"Oh, I thought I heard but. But, what?"

She stretched her lips together tightly.

"If you want to talk about something, shoot," I said.

"I don't need to talk about anything."

This was working great. I wanted to hug Suzy. "It up to you, Mom. I can talk about anything you want to talk about." I worked the potato peeler on one side of a potato.

"Actually, there is something I want to say. I want to thank you, Colette, for recommending Jake. He's quite the worker." My mom looked right at me.

I continued working on the potato. I turned it over and used the peeler on the other side. The potato skin was flying all over the sink. I didn't respond right away because I couldn't think of anything to say. I wished I hadn't recommended him. "Yeah, he's okay," I finally said.

"Anything else about him?"

"No."

"Dad and I think he's so polite." My mom emphasized so. "Always saying please and thank you."

I didn't want to talk about Jake at all. Maybe my mom knew that. Hmm. "Oh yes, he is, Mom. He even says please and thank you to me. I think that's very unusual."

"Yes. Dad and I think so too. Very unusual." She put the pork chops in the pan. "What else do you like about him?"

"I don't know."

"Something wrong, Colette?"

134

"No, I'm enjoying helping you fix dinner. I'm learning a lot."

"I'm so glad about that. Maybe you can take over some of the cooking in the future."

This was not going the way I planned. I was not about to cook for the family. I did enough work. I did dishes every night but Sunday. I worked every other Saturday at the store. I babysat. And my homework was every single night in at least one or two subjects, maybe more. Maybe I shouldn't help my mom in the kitchen. But then I couldn't put Suzy's idea into action. Suzy said her mom got sick of her quickly. "Maybe. Sure, Mom. Just what I was thinking."

"Really?"

"Really."

"Well, since you're so into cooking, you can get the asparagus ready. Wash it first and then just break the stalks."

This was going to be a long three weeks. I didn't even like asparagus much less care how it was fixed. "Sure, Mom. Where are they?"

"In the refrigerator."

Our refrigerator was in the back hall, not in the kitchen. So I could get away from my mom for a minute. I walked over to the refrigerator and stood behind the door. I had to think about my strategy. Usually I was at softball practice at this time. When I came home dinner was served. I wondered what they were doing at practice.

I brought the asparagus into the kitchen.

"Perfect," my mom said. "You're being such a help. I feel like hugging you." She put her arm around my shoulder and squeezed. "One thing I can see is that we're going to become best buddies."

I didn't move. Didn't she remember she had grounded me for three weeks?

"In fact, this grounding may turn out to be good for our relationship. Who would've guessed?" My mom turned the pork chops, wiped her hands on her apron, and smiled wider than I'd ever seen her smile.

Plan A and plan B weren't working. I needed a plan C. "Mom, I need to concentrate on the asparagus. I can't talk right now."

"Tell me when you think you can talk." She whistled as she worked at the stove.

At dinner, my mom and dad were so chatty and nice, it was sickening. They had obviously talked to each other. I lost track of what they were talking about but it sure sounded happy. They were laughing away.

"Don't you think so, Colette?" My dad asked.

"What?"

"Your mother told me that you want to do some cooking. I think that's a great idea. Don't you?"

"Of course, I do. I was fixing asparagus, wasn't I?"

Gramps was looking back and forth between my dad and me. I got the feeling the day before that Gramps was on my side but he would never say anything in front of me to my mom or dad. He said it was none of his business.

"I can't wait until tomorrow," my mom said.

"Oh, neither can I," I said.

Chapter Twenty

Secrets Can be a Burden

Suzy and I met for lunch. "Okay, give," she said, "what happened yesterday?"

"I used your idea and became my mom's little shadow."

"And?"

"And she became nervous to begin with and then I think she realized what I was doing."

"Your mom is smart."

"She is. She started talking about how much she loved me helping her in the kitchen and how our relationship was going to be stronger. Then she hugged me and said maybe I could start cooking for the family."

"Oh, boy. Tell me more."

"I peeled potatoes, snapped asparagus stalks, brought food to the table, did the dishes, and then sat in the living room with Gramps while I did my homework."

Suzy laughed. "I feel sorry for you."

"I have to say that I was really tired. I was in bed by nine o'clock."

"Can you talk on the phone?"

"They didn't say anything about the phone. But I can only talk for a half hour at a time."

"Here's my idea. You can call me when you get tired of cooking or talking with your mom. I'll try to think of a new strategy."

"Okay. I might need to give you a call." I got up from the table. "See you later."

I rode my bike to school since the weather was so perfect now. My books and folders were in a plastic bag in the rear basket. Today I took a long way home and didn't hurry; I felt free. I resisted going to the ball field behind the school because I would have started practicing, believe me.

Our garage was behind the house in an alley. I parked my bike in the garage in its spot off to the side and walked up to the house. Gramps was reading in his favorite chair in the sunroom. I walked in. "Hi, Gramps."

Gramps put the book down and motioned to a chair for me. "Sit down," he said. "How was school today?"

"It was okay."

"You're winding down for the year. Summer vacation is coming up."

"I can't wait."

"What are you going to do this summer?"

"I don't know, Gramps. I don't have any plans. I'm not old enough for driver's training so I guess I'll do nothing all summer."

"Softball?"

"Oh, yeah. I'll play softball." There was something about sitting with Gramps that always lifted my spirits. I started thinking about playing softball in the summer and how great it was going to be.

"Good. I love going to your games."

"I know. So do Aunt Florence and Rosie." I thought of something. "Say, Gramps, since you love the games so much, maybe you could talk to Mom and Dad about my grounding."

"I'm not going to interfere."

"I don't look at it that way. It's just giving your opinion."

Gramps didn't respond. His hands were on his lap.

"I remember you telling me that I should be comfortable enough at home to give my opinion. Even if I disagreed with everybody."

"Bella, you are really something." Bella was Gramp's nickname for me. It meant beautiful in Italian.

"Well, maybe you disagree with Mom and Dad on their really unfair punishment. I think you should voice that."

"One of the reasons we get along so well in the house is because I don't interfere. If I did, maybe your parents would want to move to their own place."

"I see what you mean. But maybe I could just stay with you after they move."

"Bella, Bella."

"It's just my opinion, Gramps."

"You are a very funny girl. Come here and give me a hug."

I did because that was one of my favorite things to do.

"Colette, are you around?" My mom stood in the doorway. "I've been waiting in the kitchen for you. I need help."

I wondered how she had done it all those years without me. "I hope you don't have potatoes and asparagus again."

"No, we're having more of a summer meal because it's warm. I'm making chicken salad. I need celery and onions cut up."

Great. The more I cut up onions, the more I cried. I went out to the kitchen. My mom was already frying chicken breasts. She had water on the stove for the macaroni. The celery and one big onion waited on the table for me. My mom showed me how to wash, break off the celery stalks, and then cut the celery into bite-sized pieces. And she wanted the onion diced. So that's what we talked about; celery and onions.

After we exhausted the subject of how to prepare chicken salad, my mom talked about retiring from St. Anastasia's. She had been there for so long, it wasn't the same without me there, my dad needed help, the store was busier than ever, they had plans to make the store bigger, and they needed to hire another person. I didn't have to say a word other than "Mmm, Hmm" and "I see what you mean."

There was no mention of Jake or my grounding. So the conversation was pleasant enough even though my mom was doing all the talking. This is the way the week went with me listening to my mom going back and forth about leaving her job at St. Anastasia's and both of us avoiding the subject of my grounding.

Suzy questioned me every day at lunch. "How's it going?" She would ask. "Is your mom sick of you yet?"

"Actually, I think my mom enjoys having me in the kitchen cutting up vegetables and anything else she comes up with." I said.

By the end of the week, I have to say, I really didn't know how my mom made such a good meal every day. She worked all day and then worked again in the kitchen. I mean, between the slicing and dicing, boiling water for this or that, making sure the oven was on or something frying in the frying pan, the meal came together. We had vegetables with every meal and some kind of bread like muffins or cornbread or rolls. And everything had to be done at the same time. Of course, I didn't tell my mom that I was amazed how she put it all together but I was.

At lunch, Laurie Zastrow asked me when I was coming back to play softball. I said, "Hopefully, soon."

Suzy told me that everyone on the team wondered why I wasn't there and if I was sick. "I didn't tell them that you were grounded because I didn't want everybody making up stories about what you had done," Suzy said.

"Thanks, Suzy," I said. "I appreciate it." I knew she was dying to ask me again what the story was but she didn't. I guess I appreciated that too. "I'm in school so they know I'm not sick." I didn't know exactly what my mom told the coach.

"That's true. I'm surprised people aren't asking you questions. Anyway, we missed you at practice."

"Do you really think I'd rather be slicing and dicing vegetables in the kitchen while my mom talks about leaving St. Anastasia's?"

"No, I don't think so." She laughed. "The game wasn't the same without you cheering me on."

"Tell me everything about the game." Suzy did such a good job telling me about the game that I felt like I was there. She told me I don't have to worry about losing my job at third base. Suzy was becoming a good friend. Someday maybe I'd tell her the whole story.

I wasn't working on Saturday so I slept as late as I could. It was almost noon when I got up. Gramps was reading in the sunroom when I came downstairs. He put down the book. "Sit down," he said. "I was waiting for you for lunch."

"That's nice, Gramps. I like our Saturday lunches."

"What would you like today? Grilled cheese or peanut butter and jelly with soup?"

"I'll take grilled cheese."

"Me too. Why don't we go into the kitchen?"

Gramps stood up. He waited until I went out of the door first. Gramps would never walk through a door before a girl. He thought men should open doors for women. If all the seats on a bus were taken, the men should stand up and let the women sit, Gramps would say. He called himself old-fashioned. Old-fashioned or not, he was the perfect gentleman.

Gramps got the grilled cheese ready. I picked out vegetable beef soup and put it in a pan. Gramps and I stood together fixing lunch; it seemed like the perfectly natural thing to do. After lunch, Gramps asked me if I wanted to look at the old photo albums.

We sat together on the living room couch. Gramps took out all the photo albums. "Should we start at the beginning?" We looked at Gramp's wedding picture. There was my Grandma Rose and Gramps looking so young and happy. "I knew she was the one the first time I saw her," he said.

I nodded. Gramps always said that when we talked about Grandma Rose. We looked at pictures of my mom and Aunt Florence down by the river. There was a picture of Uncle Daniel pointing at a paddle wheeler. Another picture showed Grandma Rose and the three children on the front steps of the house.

Gramps took out the picture of Uncle Daniel in his army uniform. Gramps stared at it for a minute before he handed it to me. "I can't believe it's been twenty two years."

"I feel like I know him from our talks, Gramps."

He patted my arm. "You're a great listener."

"Remember when you told me I should be a psychiatrist?"

"I remember. Who knows, maybe you will. You helped all of us."

I thought about all the things that happened three years ago. "I learned a lot about the family."

"Secrets can be a burden for people," he said.

"What?"

"I said secrets can be a burden for people. I'm so grateful you got us talking."

"It wasn't just me, Gramps."

"You're right. Everyone in the family wanted the secrets out. But you got it going."

"I guess I did because you're my family and I wanted to know what had happened to you in the past."

"I feel that way too. I want to know what's going on with my family." Gramps hadn't taken his eyes off me since he started describing secrets as a burden.

I looked down at the picture of my Uncle Daniel on my lap. I felt my face getting warm and shifted in the seat. "Actually, I forgot, I've got homework to do. You know how the end of the year is." I put the picture back in the open album. "We can look at the rest of these later," I said as I stood up.

"Okay, Bella. Give me a hug." His arms were open like they always were for little Rosie. "Remember, your cousin Daniel is coming tonight for dinner."

"That's right, I forgot."

"Florence, Mike, and Rosie are coming tonight too."

Great. I'd be subjected to Uncle Mike's stares all night. "Gotta go."

I could not look Gramps in the eye. He knew I was lying about the whole whiskey deal and I knew he wanted me to tell him what happened. I didn't know how to do that without having lots more questions coming my way. So, contrary to my personality, I cut Gramps off and went upstairs.

Chapter Twenty One
Daniel's Visit

My mom came home at five o'clock. "Colette, I need help," she said.

She was in the kitchen getting hamburgers and french fries ready; our usual Saturday meal. "Could you peel the potatoes and slice them for french fries?"

"I will." I had no trouble peeling potatoes; I felt like I could do it in my sleep. And I loved my mom's home-made french fries so I didn't mind that either. I wondered if Gramps had told her about our afternoon conversation.

"Did you remember that Daniel is coming and Florence, Mike, and Rosie?"

"Gramps told me. When are they coming here?"

"About six. Daniel stopped by the store for a few minutes before going to Florence's." My mom made the hamburger patties and put them on a plate with wax paper between them. "I figure two hamburgers each for the men and one for you, Florence, and me. That's eleven. I'll make twelve and that should take care of it."

"We'll need a lot of french fries. What else are we having?"

"I got some cans of baked beans. I didn't have time to make anything else."

"What's for dessert?"

"Florence made two strawberry rhubarb pies."

"Yum."

Daniel came a little before six. We hadn't seen him since Christmas vacation. Gramps gave him a big hug and told him how good he looked. He had finished his third year at Madison.

"What are you doing this summer, Colette?" Daniel asked.

"I don't know. I really don't have anything planned."

"How about camp? I used to do that in high school."

"Camp sounds wonderful. It would get me out of the house."

Daniel laughed. "You need to get out of the house, do you?"

"Yeah, I do. Especially since I'm grounded."

Daniel looked back and forth from Gramps to my mom. The doorbell rang and opened. Rosie came running in and Gramps swept her up. Aunt Florence and Uncle Mike followed. My dad pulled the car into the garage. My mom said, "Good, John's home."

My dad lit the coals in the grill. Aunt Florence went right into the kitchen and put on an apron. That meant I didn't have to be in the kitchen. Hallelujah.

In a half hour we were sitting at the table with the hamburgers, buns, french fries, and baked beans in front of us. We waited for Gramps to say "Grace." "Bless us oh Lord...," he began. All of us including Daniel joined in. Gramps added his usual, "Thank you, Lord, for our food and for each other."

The food was passed around and the conversation centered on Daniel and his plans for the summer and for his last year at Madison. I just sat back and listened. No one asked me about softball or my plans for the summer.

The more I thought about Daniel's idea of camp, the more I liked it. "I'm thinking about going to camp this summer," I said. I had just interrupted the conversation about what classes Daniel had left. He didn't seem to mind. In fact, he had a half-smile on his face.

"That's a good idea. I really liked camp in the summer," Daniel said.

"I'd like that experience too. In fact, I've always wanted to go to Lake Itasca."

"Oh, you should," Aunt Florence said. "I loved it. It's the beginning of the Mississippi River. You can walk across it."

My mom and dad looked more than a little surprised since I had never said a word about Lake Itasca or camping for that matter.

"Do you think everybody in Minnesota should see Lake Itasca?" I asked.

Both Daniel and Aunt Florence nodded. "I do," Daniel said. "And the Boundary Waters too. Everybody should see that."

"And the North Shore. Don't forget about Lake Superior," Aunt Florence said.

"I wonder why we've never gone camping or taken advantage of all the great places in Minnesota. Mom and Dad, why haven't we?" I asked.

"Well, because..." my mom said. "I don't know why."

"We have a business," my dad said. "I can't leave it for a week."

Gramps hadn't said a word but now he chimed in. "I felt that way too, John. I wish I had taken more time off."

My dad had taken two weeks off when we went to Italy. Last summer, when Aunt Sofia visited, my dad closed the store both Saturdays that they were here.

My mom had started clearing the table. "Florence, will you help me?" She asked.

"Mike, I could use some help too," my dad said. My dad cleaned the grill right after dinner. He went to the back porch with Uncle Mike.

Aunt Florence and my mom finished clearing the table and then disappeared into the kitchen. They had to make whipped cream for the pies. Gramps was busy making sure that Rosie didn't climb the stairs or anything else that she could fall from. That left Daniel and I alone.

"I'm glad you like school," I said.

"I do like school. It's so different from high school." He combed his fingers through his thick, black hair. "I have to ask you something."

"Go ahead." The two of us were standing in the living room. He was tall and thin but not skinny. He had dark, where are the pupil, eyes like Gramps and me.

"What did you do?"

"Didn't they tell you?"

"No."

"Well. I'm not going to tell you either because I didn't do anything. They just think I did and that bugs me." I sat down on the couch.

Daniel sat in a chair. He leaned forward. "Why don't you tell them the truth then?"

"I can't. It involves other people."

"I understand. You don't want to be a tattletale."

"I'm not a tattletale."

"I want to ask you another question."

"Okay."

"What do you think of Jake? I met him at the store today."

"I don't know." I rubbed my hands together.

"Do you like him?"

"He's okay. What do you think of him?"

"There's something I don't like about him."

"Lots of kids think he's cool."

"Oh, that explains it."

"Explains what?" Aunt Florence asked. She stopped in front of Daniel and me.

"Nothing. Colette and I were just talking about the end of the school year."

"Okay. Let's have dessert." Aunt Florence carried one of her strawberry rhubarb pies to the table. My mom followed with the other one.

"Delicious, Florence. Your pie is wonderful," Gramps said. "One of my favorites."

"Thanks." She gave a little bow.

Daniel left at nine o'clock, shortly after Aunt Florence, Mike, and Rosie. Gramps hugged Daniel and kissed him on both cheeks. "Godspeed, Daniel," Gramps said.

"Come back soon," my mom said. She gave him a kiss on the cheek.

"Before the end of the summer," he said. "Bye, Colette. Have a good summer."

"I will. Bye."

"Come help me in the kitchen," my mom said.

All the dessert plates were in a pile waiting to be washed. There were plates in the drying rack that my mom was putting away. Soapy water was in the dishpan. I didn't think this would be the time to ask my mom why we didn't have a dishwasher.

"Do you really want to go to Lake Itasca?" My mom asked.

"Well, Aunt Florence told me how great it was. So did Daniel. I guess I do want to go there."

"Maybe I can talk your dad into taking three or four days off and we can go this summer. Gramps has never been there and neither have I."

"That would really be fun." I couldn't believe it. Maybe she wasn't all that mad at me.

"How about camping? Do you want to go camping?"

"No, I'm not the camping type. I like a bed."

"Good. So do I."

Chapter Twenty Two

God's Country

The next day at the Diner all the talk was about Daniel. "I liked talking to him about all the wonderful places he's been to in Minnesota," I said.

"That was interesting," my mom agreed.

"Especially the camping part," my dad said. "I didn't know you loved camping, Colette."

"I thought I did for a minute when he was talking about going up to the Boundary Waters this summer and canoeing." I took a bite of bacon. It was so good. "He called it 'God's Country.' Even though I'd like to see it, it seems like a lot of work."

"It is. You have to bring in all the food, make a fire every night, and pitch a tent," my mom said.

"He said it's wonderful sitting by the fire at night and looking at the stars."

"Yes, it is wonderful," my dad said. "I went there in college with friends. You also have to carry the canoe from lake to lake. That's called portaging."

"How do you know where to go?" I asked.

"There are maps. But it's a huge area with many, many lakes. You can get lost if you're not careful."

"What was your favorite part?"

"The quiet while we were canoeing. The air and water are so clean. It's exhilarating to take in a deep breath."

Gramps said, "I think I'm too old to portage and camp but I would like to go to Lake Itasca."

"Me too, Gramps," I said.

When we got home, my mom and dad took me into the sunroom and closed the door.

"Sit down, Colette," my dad said. "Your mother and I have decided something."

"We're talking about the grounding," my mom said.

I sat up straighter. Had they found out something?

"I asked parents at school how much time is appropriate for grounding. They all agreed three weeks is really severe. And you didn't lie about where you were going, sneak out of the house, do something dangerous, or anything like that."

"No, I didn't do anything like that. I wouldn't do any of those things."

"I know. And we've never grounded you before so we kind of went overboard."

"Not completely overboard. Something happened at Florence and Mike's. We're not getting the whole story," my dad said.

I thought about saying maybe Mike just thought water was put in his whiskey and then I thought better of it. If I had to guess, my mom was more on my side than my dad. So it was Mom, Aunt Florence, and probably Gramps in my corner. Uncle Mike and Dad in the other corner. I waited to see what would come next.

My mom looked at my dad. "John, I thought we agreed."

Oh, this was interesting. I bet Gramps or Aunt Florence said something to my mom and then she asked people at school if it was unfair.

"We did agree, Gemma. I'm just saying we weren't totally out of line."

"Okay, I hear you. But that's not why we brought Colette in here. I might as well just say it. Your grounding was much too much." She looked at my dad for a minute before continuing. "You've been very helpful to me in the kitchen and done it without complaining. I appreciate that."

I really didn't have a choice. I couldn't go to softball practice and I didn't want to sit up in my room. I crossed my fingers.

"Your dad and I have compromised here. He wanted you to finish the three weeks. I thought two weeks was plenty of time." My mom stood next to my dad in their usual united front. "Anyway, we decided that your grounding will be over on Saturday. You're working that day but you can go out Saturday night if you want to. There, that's it."

I was stunned. I didn't know what brought this all about but I wasn't arguing, believe me. "Thank you," I said.

"No more lying," my dad said.

"I won't."

"I'll still need help in the kitchen this week," my mom said.

"Sure, I can do that." I was not going to mind chopping vegetables or peeling potatoes one bit. I could practice next week and then the championship game was on Saturday, the day after our last day of school.

Monday was Memorial Day so we had the day off of school. The store was closed too. We went for a drive to the cemetery where Grandma Rose and Uncle Daniel were buried. This was something we did every year. A lot of people were visiting graves and putting flowers and flags there.

The two graves were next to each other. Gramps went once a week all year, rain or shine. He knelt down between the graves. He wiped his eyes and so did my mom. She had made two bouquets of iris and peonies from our backyard. She placed a bouquet on each grave. We said the "Our Father" together. I thought the "Our Father" was a versatile prayer because we always said it at Mass, before every game, and even at the cemetery.

On the way home we talked about Grandma Rose and Uncle Daniel. The more my family talked, the more I wished I had known them both. It was hard to believe that I didn't since Grandma Rose and Uncle Daniel were so much a part of my family's lives.

Chapter Twenty Three

An Invitation

At school on Tuesday, I told Suzy about the change in my grounding.

"Maybe my idea really did work," she said. "I think your mom got sick of you being every place she went."

"Maybe." I didn't think that was the reason, but since she thought her plan was such a great plan, I didn't want to hurt her feelings. Anyway, we had talked about my grounding every day without her even knowing the reason.

"How about coming over on Saturday?"

"That would be great."

The rest of the week flew by with our teachers finishing up lessons, me preparing vegetables every afternoon in the kitchen, and doing homework every evening after dinner. I couldn't wait for summer vacation.

I overheard Sam and Sally talking about some big party coming up over the weekend. I think they wanted me to hear about it because I wasn't invited.

It was my weekend to work at the store. I hadn't said a word to Jake since he came over when I was babysitting. I got to the store at ten o'clock. Jake was already there. I planned on working in the soda fountain all day and paying no attention to Jake or his friends for that matter. I went into the backroom to get my apron. I walked over to the soda fountain. Jake stood by the counter, waiting.

"Colette, I have to talk to you," he said.

"Why?"

"Because I feel so bad about what happened." Jake tried to look really sincere. I wasn't buying it.

"I'm sure," I said. I took strawberries and pineapple topping out of the small refrigerator and filled the metal containers half-way.

Jake hadn't moved.

"Aren't you busy?" I asked. I couldn't believe I said that to him but the last two weeks had been awful. My parents didn't trust me, Uncle Mike didn't want me babysitting, and

I was really sick of helping with dinner. Plus, I hadn't been practicing so I wouldn't be ready for the big game.

He leaned over the counter. "I just wanted to thank you for not telling on me. I really appreciate it." He rapped on the counter and walked away.

The day went by quickly with many customers in the soda fountain. My mom switched places with me when my hands got too cold or I needed a break. It was a welcome change.

I was almost done with my work for the day. I still had to put away anything that needed to be in the refrigerator. I had to clean the containers and wipe them dry. I would call Suzy as soon as I got home.

"Colette, can you watch the register for a minute?" My mom said.

"Sure."

Jake came over to the register. "One more thing," he said.

"I'm not checking out any cigarettes for you, if that's what you want."

"I don't have any cigarettes. I just wanted to tell you that I'm having an end of the year party tonight if you want to come."

"I have plans already."

"Sam invited some of her friends too. Just letting you know. It starts at eight."

This was the party Sam and Sally were talking about all week in school. "No thanks. Not tonight."

At dinner that night, my mom and dad went on and on about Jake. He was such a good worker, he was so polite and pleasant, he was just great. It really bugged me. "He's far from perfect," I said.

"I thought you liked him, Colette," my dad said.

"You act like he's perfect. I work hard too."

"You do work hard and we love having you work with us," my mom said.

"The customers love Colette," Gramps said.

"Thanks, Gramps. Anyway, I'm going over to Suzy's for a couple of hours." I got up from the table. "I'll do the dishes now." I couldn't wait to get out of the house.

"Do you want a ride?" My mom asked.

"No, I'll take my bike. I'll be home at nine or nine thirty." Suzy lived about four blocks away from me. I rode my bike, thinking that I never wanted to be grounded again.

"C'mon in, Colette." Suzy opened the door.

"Hi, Colette," Mrs. Malone said. "Good to see you again."

"Let's go to my room," Suzy said.

She told me all about practice and how the team couldn't wait for me to come back. "Nobody can play third base like you do. The coach tried a couple different girls. They couldn't make the throw to first. He'll be happy since the championship game is next Saturday."

"I really have to practice." I thought of something else. "Have you ever gone to Lake Itasca?"

"We went last summer."

"Did you like it?"

"I liked it and I didn't like it."

"Tell me what you liked."

"Well, it was really cool walking across the beginning of the Mississippi River. That was great. And it's pretty too. We camped so I was in a tent with my whole family. That's what I didn't like. It was hard to sleep so my mom and dad were really crabby by the time we got home. Matt and Jim complained about the heat, the mosquitoes, their sleeping bags, and everything else. They didn't want to hike or look at the beautiful wild flowers. They didn't like the food my mom brought."

"What did your parents do about all their complaining?"

"At one point my dad told them to shut up, which he never does. He said they were very spoiled."

"Did they stop?"

"Not completely, but it was better. I guess we were all happy to get home. I mean, how many wild orchids can you look at?"

I was so relaxed sitting in Suzy's room that I thought I could tell her about why I was grounded. "If I tell you something, do you promise not to tell anyone?"

"I promise."

"I mean even your parents."

"I don't tell my parents everything."

"Good. This has to stay between you and me." I told her why I was grounded. She couldn't believe that Jake came over to Aunt Florence's when I was babysitting. She thought that was really strange. She was open-mouthed when I told her about him stealing some of my uncle's whiskey and then filling it with water. I told her that I couldn't tell on him because he works at the store.

"So what, Colette. You don't owe him anything."

"I'm not a tattletale."

"I know you aren't. But you should tell your parents."

"The grounding is over now so I'm going to forget it."

"That would be hard for me to do. Your uncle thinks you stole some of his whiskey."

"I know. He doesn't want me babysitting."

"Do you like Jake?"

"I used to, but not anymore." I told her about how my parents raved about him.

"That would bug me too. Especially since we both know what a jerk he is."

"I agree."

"He swaggers around school, smiling at all the girls. He's conceited."

If I told her about telling my dad to hire him at the store, she would have thought I was really dumb.

"I'm not completely surprised by the whiskey deal," Suzy said. Jake and his friends go down by the river a lot. I bet they drink down there."

"Maybe."

"There's a big party tonight at O'Malley's."

"I heard about it too. Jake talked about it at the store." I didn't say that he had invited me.

"Sam asked me to come."

"She did?"

"She just mentioned it to some of the girls on the team. She said the whole boy's baseball team was going too. You weren't there so that's why she didn't invite you."

"Oh, yeah."

"Sam said her parents are gone overnight. She was really excited about it."

"Did you want to go?"

"No, not really. I'm sure they'll be drinking."

"You're not supposed to if you're on the school teams."

"I don't think that's going to stop them."

I looked at my watch. It was after eight. I don't know why I kept thinking about the party. I couldn't get it off my mind. Maybe because Jake invited me but Sam didn't and she even invited Suzy. I wondered if Sally was there and what she told her parents. They would never let her go to a party if they knew the parents were gone. Well, there was nothing I could do about it.

"What if I make a big error?" Suzy asked.

"What?" I had no idea what Suzy was talking about.

"I was just talking about the game next Saturday. I know you're not nervous but I am."

We had won six of our eight games during the season, the same as Lake City. It was not going to be an easy game. "I'm nervous too. I have to practice hard this week." We had practices the rest of the week. I looked at my watch again. It was eight thirty. I just didn't feel comfortable anymore so I started fidgeting in the chair.

"Something wrong?"

"No, no. Nothing's wrong. I just have to go home now." I stood up.

"Already?"

"I told my mom I'd be home by nine at the latest. So I better go." I couldn't tell if she was upset. I walked to the front door. "I had a great time. I'll see you on Monday."

"See you Monday."

I hoped I didn't hurt Suzy's feelings, specially since she had made a place for me at the lunch table and never pushed me to tell her anything. But for some reason, I felt that I had to go. I guess it was all the talk about drinking. Sally never drank alcohol and I had to make sure that she wasn't in trouble.

Chapter Twenty Four
Jake's Party

Instead of going home, I rode my bike over to Jake's house. I didn't know how I was going to walk into the house since Sam hadn't invited me. I figured I had almost an hour to make sure Sally was okay and still get home by nine thirty.

I turned the corner onto Jake's street. There was no place to park on the street; all the parking places were filled with cars. There were kids hanging around on the front lawn and a few bikes next to the front steps. I leaned my bike against the front steps.

I took in a deep breath and walked into the house. The living room was filled with probably forty or fifty kids dancing and singing along to The Beach Boys. It really was wall to wall kids. I couldn't move.

Where was Sally? I looked around. I didn't see her but, to tell you the truth, it was hard to see anyone because there was only one light on. I bumped into a girl I didn't know. "Excuse me. Sorry."

"Watch where you're going," the girl said as she flipped her blonde hair around to her back. She turned away from me.

I looked around for Sam or anybody from my softball team. Most of the kids were juniors and seniors. I saw John, Sally's brother, sitting on a couch next to a girl. Maybe Sally wasn't here. I could barely move. "Excuse me," I said as walked into the kitchen. If she wasn't there I was going home. Jake was in the kitchen with several girls surrounding him. The girl he went to prom with was right next to him, hanging on him and his every word.

"Sport, c'mon in," Jake said. "We work together," he told the group around him. "Her parents own Rossini and McGiver's."

"I hate to interrupt, but is Sally here?"

"Yep. She's here."

"Where is she?"

"I don't know. There are some kids in the back yard." He took a big drink out of the plastic glass in his hand. "By the way, help yourself. There's punch in the dining room."

"Thanks." I walked into the dining room. Sally and Sam and a couple other girls from the softball team stood next to the dining room table. There was a big bowl of punch in the center of the table.

"Oh my Gawd," Sally said. "Look who's here. Sam, did you invite her?" Sally took a big gulp from her glass.

"No. No, I didn't," Sam said. She went to fill her glass from the punch bowl. "Anyone?"

Sally handed over her glass. Sam filled it. "Are you crashing the party, Colette?" She took another big gulp.

Maybe this was a really bad idea. Why was I so worried about Sally anyway? She didn't worry about me, believe me. "I was invited."

"Really? Who invited you?" Sam asked.

"Your brother."

"Jake? I don't think so," Sam said. "You know what. I'm going to ask him."

Sam walked out to the kitchen. Sally shifted her weight back and forth. "I thought you were grounded, Colette."

"Not anymore."

"That's good, I suppose."

"Yeah, it's good." It was the weirdest thing but Sally and I used to talk for hours. We never ran out of conversation. Now, the two of us were reduced to a couple of uncomfortable words. I looked at my watch. It was almost nine thirty.

"Have to be home?"

"No, I mean, yeah, I have to be home."

"I'm staying overnight so I don't have to worry."

Sam came back into the dining room. "Jake said he invited her. Have some punch. It's good, isn't it, Sally?"

Sam handed me a glass of punch. I took a drink. It was terrible. "What's in the punch?" I asked.

"You don't want to know."

There were a couple other girls from the softball team standing around. "I better get going," I said. I had never known Sally to even drink a beer but I couldn't do a thing about the whole situation.

"Bye," Sally said. She looked in the kitchen. I looked too. Jake and his old girlfriend were hugging and kissing. Maybe she was his girlfriend again since the prom. Sally took a big gulp from her glass. "Fill 'er up," she said to Sam.

"Sal, how many glasses have you had? I asked. I wondered how many people were staying overnight.

"None of your business."

"I think you should leave," I said.

"Why?"

"You've had too much to drink." Sally still liked Jake, that was obvious. I had to get her out of there.

"Why don't you leave? Right now," Sam said. She stood in front of me. "I said go."

The phone rang. Jake picked it up, listened, and then hung up. "Everybody out," he said. "The neighbor said if people don't leave, he's calling the police." He turned on the lights in the living room, turned off the music, and yelled, "Out. Everyone out." Then he went into the back yard and yelled, "The party's over. Go home."

"Sally's staying over," Sam said.

"No, she's not. I said everyone."

"We've had parties before. What's she supposed to do?"

"Go home."

Sally looked stunned. "I can't go home like this," she said. "My mom will kill me."

"I've got an idea. Sally, come with me," I said. We walked out of the house into the front yard.

I grabbed my bike and started walking with Sally on the sidewalk. It was after ten o'clock and so my parents were probably wondering where I was. I bet my mom called Suzy's house when I didn't get home by nine thirty. Suzy would have told her that I left a long time ago. I bet my dad wished he hadn't agreed to change my grounding. Sally and I went to the end of the block, turned the corner, and there we were in front of Aunt Florence's house.

Chapter Twenty Five

Aunt Florence to the Rescue

I knocked on the door, hoping that Uncle Mike wouldn't answer it. I had told Sally that Aunt Florence would know what to do. Uncle Mike opened the door and stood in disbelief. "Colette, what the heck?"

"Can we come in?"

"I guess so. Florence, we have visitors," he said.

Aunt Florence was in the living room watching the news. She stood up and came over to the two of us. "Are you in trouble, Colette? What happened?"

"Aunt Florence, will you call my parents? I was supposed to be home about an hour ago."

"Do you want to tell me what's going on?"

"Can we sit?"

"Sure, sit down."

"There was a big party tonight at O'Malley's. A neighbor called and said he was going to call the police if people didn't leave. So we left."

"Have you been drinking?"

"No.

Aunt Florence looked at Sally. "Sally, have you been drinking?"

Sally looked down at the floor. "Yes."

"She didn't know the punch was spiked," I said.

"Okay. I'll have to call her parents too."

Sally groaned. "My parents are going to be really mad."

"I'll explain. It could have been a lot worse if the police had come. Excuse me," Aunt Florence said. She walked out to the kitchen where her phone hung on the wall.

Uncle Mike stood with his arms crossed. He made me really uncomfortable. I didn't know what to say and obviously he didn't either because neither of us said a word. I suppose he thought I wasn't being totally truthful again. "Uncle Mike, would you get us some water? We're both really thirsty," I said

When Uncle Mike left the room, Sally leaned into me. "I can't thank you enough for telling your aunt that I had no idea about the punch," she said. "I owe you one."

Uncle Mike came back with the water for us. "Was O'Malley the one who took my whiskey?"

I took in a deep breath and said, "Yes."

"Why was he here when you were babysitting?"

"He came over. I didn't ask him. I don't even like him."

Sally had been staring at me. I hoped she didn't think that I was chasing Jake. I know she wondered why he invited me to the party and to tell you the truth, I did too. Maybe he was afraid I would tell my parents about the whiskey or Musolf's.

Aunt Florence came into the living room. "Okay, here's what's going on. I talked to both your parents. I'm going to drive both of you home."

"Are my parents mad?" Sally asked.

"They're a little mad. John was home so he told them the party had broken up," Aunt Florence said. "Your mom called O'Malley's to see if you were still staying over and Sam had no idea where you were."

"Oh, I bet they were worried," Sally said. She looked like she was going to cry.

"They were worried. They wanted to know if you'd been drinking. I assured them that you didn't know the punch was spiked."

Aunt Florence seemed to know what to do. I suppose that came from her years as a nursing supervisor. She sure was organized.

"Now, Colette. Your parents were worried too. They had called Suzy's and she had no idea where you were."

"I suppose I'm grounded again."

"I will be too," Sally said.

"Okay, let's go. The car is in the garage," Aunt Florence said. "Mike, I'll drop them off and come right home."

"Just a minute, Florence," Uncle Mike said. "Can I talk to you in the kitchen?"

Aunt Florence was back in the living room in no time. "C'mon, girls."

Sally grabbed me as we walked through the back yard to the garage. She squeezed my arm and whispered, "Thank you."

Aunt Florence dropped off Sally and waited until her parents opened the door. "Mike said that Jake was the one who took the whiskey. Is that true?"

"That's true."

"Okay. Mike is calling your parents now so they'll know by the time you get home." Aunt Florence looked at me. "I asked your mom about taking you up to St. Paul tomorrow. She wasn't sure. I didn't know about Jake when I asked her. She may want you to stay home."

"Sure. I'd like to go." If I stayed at home, I'd be grounded for sure. I'd probably have to chop up vegetables all afternoon.

"It's up to your parents." We pulled up to my house. It was almost eleven. "Here we are. Maybe I'll see you tomorrow."

"Thanks for helping us tonight."

"You're welcome." She patted my arm. "You better go."

My parents both opened the door. "Colette, let's go sit in the living room," my mom said. "We were very worried about you. I called Suzy's at ten o'clock and she said you left long before nine. She was puzzled about where you could be because you didn't mention going anywhere else."

"It was a last minute decision. I didn't plan on going to the party."

"Okay. Then why did you go there?"

"I thought Sally might be in trouble." I was glad I went to the party but my parents wouldn't understand that.

"I didn't know you were even talking to Sally. Why did you think she might be in trouble?"

"I just had a feeling. I'm sorry you were worried about me. I went to the party because I was worried about Sally. That's the truth."

"Uncle Mike called," my dad said. "He said Jake was the one who took the whiskey. Why didn't you tell us that?"

"I don't know."

"You should tell us things, Colette. You were grounded for two weeks because of him. Why?"

"I don't know. I just can't talk anymore. Please don't ask me any more questions."

My mom went over to stand next to my dad's chair. "John, why don't we go to bed? You're getting upset, I'm getting upset, and I bet Colette is upset too."

My dad started to say something. My mom put her hand on his shoulder. "We can talk more tomorrow. Let's go to bed."

"Aunt Florence said I was going to St. Paul with her tomorrow. Am I?" I really didn't think I could take any more grilling. I wondered if Sally was being grilled by her parents.

"Florence asked me if you could go with her."

"Do you think that's a good idea?" My dad said.

"I didn't know about Jake when she asked. Do you want to go, Colette?"

"Yes."

"Okay. Then I want you to talk to us when you get back," my mom said.

"I'll be firing Jake tomorrow," my dad said.

"Can I go to bed now?" I asked.

"Go to bed. We have nine o'clock Mass in the morning"

My mom woke me at eight fifteen. She told me Aunt Florence would pick me up at ten o'clock. I was glad I got to ride in the car up to St. Paul, eat in the wonderful River Room at Dayton's, and who knows what else with Aunt Florence.

Gramps walked right next to me all the way to the church. He asked me about the end of school, summer plans, working at the store; everything but the party the night before. I didn't want to talk about it anyway. He put his arm around me and to tell you the truth, I wanted to cry because I couldn't stand the thought of Gramps being disappointed in me.

Mass was the same as usual with people standing, sitting, kneeling, saying prayers, and singing along with the off-key sopranos. And then, as luck would have it, Father Walsh's sermon was about the effects of lying and dishonesty on the family. He talked about rebuilding trust after it had been lost. I could have sworn he was talking to me.

At the back of the church, Sally waited for me. "Thanks, again, for getting me out of there. We'll talk later."

"Good. I'd like that." I wanted to say I've really missed you.

Aunt Florence tapped me on the shoulder. "Ready?" She said.

"I'm ready for the River Room's popovers."

Chapter Twenty Six

St. Paul

Aunt Florence was very chatty on the drive to St. Paul. The drive was a little over an hour and it was filled with really pretty sights. There were wonderful farms and planted fields of corn, wheat, and other crops. The crops weren't very high yet since it was only the beginning of June but they looked so green and I loved their perfect rows. The hills were rolling so you could see far in the distance. We saw cows munching and horses running in the fields. I couldn't get enough of it.

Aunt Florence said we should come back in August when the corn would be taller than us. We drove through Hastings, another cool town on the Mississippi. There were big, old mansions with turrets to look at that Aunt Florence and I loved. Three rivers came together in Hastings; the

Mississippi, the St. Croix, and the Vermillion. If we were lucky, we would see eagles circling.

So the conversation was pleasant on the way to St. Paul and not a word was said about the events of the night before. We pulled up to Dayton's Department Store and Aunt Florence parked underneath the store. Soon we stood waiting to be seated at the River Room.

There were white tablecloths on the tables and pretty chandeliers hanging from the ceiling. It wasn't bright in the restaurant so I had to blink until my eyes got used to the darkness. Aunt Florence and I sat at a round table for two. The waitress brought over popovers on a china plate. There was a little metal dish filled with whipped butter.

"Go ahead, Colette. I bet you're hungry."

I was hungry since I hadn't eaten yet. I broke off some of the popover and buttered it. It melted immediately. I bit into it and thought I was in heaven. It was that good.

Usually I ordered Quiche Lorraine at the River Room but Aunt Florence said I should try their chicken pot pie. She said it was delicious. Well, Aunt Florence talked me into it and I tell you it was the best decision I ever made. The chicken pot pie was more than delicious and when I added popovers melting in my mouth, I had to say that the River Room was my favorite place to eat.

We walked out of the restaurant and through the women's clothes area. "Do you want to look for a new dress?" Three years ago Aunt Florence and I came to St. Paul and ate at the River Room. After lunch, I talked Aunt Florence into buying the most fabulous red dress ever.

Aunt Florence laughed. "No, I don't need another dress. Although my red dress is Mike's favorite, so thank you." She gave a little curtsy. "Should we go to the Dairy Queen for a malt?"

"Sure." I had never turned down a Dairy Queen in my life.

"How about the Monument to eat it?"

"Okay." We had slurped our malts at the Monument three years before while Aunt Florence told me about her son, Daniel.

"Your choice. Should we drive down Summit Avenue on our way to the Dairy Queen?"

"Sure. You know it's my favorite street in St. Paul." Aunt Florence was being really, really nice. To tell you the truth,

I couldn't believe how nice she was. I wondered why she hadn't asked me about last night.

We drove by the Cathedral, the big church in St. Paul, and we were on Summit Avenue. Even though Hastings had some wonderful houses to look at, Summit won, hands down. It was mile after mile of huge houses, some churches and schools, the Governor's Mansion, and people jogging down the center boulevard. What I liked was that every house was unique. Aunt Florence and I liked so many of the houses that we really couldn't pick a favorite. She told me every house had a story all its own.

We went over the Lake Street Bridge; not my favorite thing to do, believe me. To call it rickety was an understatement because the whole bridge shook and shuddered if a bus went over it. Aunt Florence paid no attention to the state of the bridge because she was too busy droning on and on about the Mississippi River. We got our two strawberry malts at the Dairy Queen and then drove back over the Lake Street Bridge. I hung onto both of our malts as we shook along.

Aunt Florence turned onto the River Drive and the shaking stopped. Within a couple of minutes we were at the

Monument. The Monument was a memorial to the World War One soldiers from St. Paul and Ramsey County. It was a tall, simple cross with benches surrounding it and it had a great view of the river.

"Should we sit, Colette?" Aunt Florence asked. "I need to sit to drink my malt."

"Yeah, I do too." We both sipped our malts.

"Ooh, that's good," Aunt Florence said. She looked at me. "You know that I didn't bring you up here just to eat at the River Room and sip our malts at the Monument."

"I know."

"Why do you think we're here?"

"You want to know about last night."

"Yes. That's part of it."

"Okay. You can ask me questions." I took a long drink from the straw.

"Let me start with this. Colette, you're my only niece. I love you very much and I don't like to see you sad or worried. Three years ago, you listened to me pour out my heart about a painful time in my life right in this same spot. I can't thank you enough for that."

"I didn't mind. In fact, I was glad to listen."

"I know. Because that's the way you are." She took in a deep breath. "Let me tell you what that meant to me. It changed my life. We found my son, Daniel, and I'm forever grateful for that. But it changed my life in other ways too. I don't think I would have met Mike and then Rosie wouldn't be here either."

"Do you really think that?"

"Yes, I do. A great weight was lifted off of me when I was able to talk about Daniel. I could start to live my life and actually be happy." Aunt Florence sipped her malt.

I couldn't think of anything to say. I took another drink of my malt and looked down at the ground. I never thought it would be hard to talk about things but I didn't know how to start.

"As I found and our whole family found out three years ago, it's much healthier to talk about things."

"I don't want anybody to be disappointed in me."

"Okay. Now we're getting somewhere. Everyone makes mistakes. It's better to come clean. You told Mike that Jake stole his whiskey. Let's start there. How did that happen?"

I told Aunt Florence about Jake coming into the house uninvited and then taking some whiskey and filling the bottle with water. "I screamed at him and told him to leave and that woke up Rosie."

"We came home shortly after that. Why did you lie?"

"I thought you'd think that I told him to come over. And I'm not a tattletale."

"Okay. But why would you take a punishment like grounding for him? Does he have something else over your head?"

"I don't know if I would say that."

"There must be something because you're protecting him. Do you like him?"

"Not anymore."

"But you used to like him? Is that why you recommended him for the job?"

"I guess."

"What happened between you and Sally?"

I told Aunt Florence about Sally thinking she was going on a date with Jake and Jake sitting with me. "I was part of a lie to Mrs. Reynolds and my mom. I felt bad about that but Sally was my best friend so I thought I was helping her."

194

"You told Sally you would go to the movie with her so her mom wouldn't know that Jake was meeting her. You went out on a limb for her. What did she get mad about?"

"She accused me of trying to steal Jake away from her."

"Were you?"

"No. I didn't know what she was talking about. So Sally wouldn't talk to me at school and I had no one to talk to at lunch."

Aunt Florence patted my arm. "That's so hard."

"Sally started hanging around with Jake's sister, Sam. After a while, I realized that she wasn't going to get over it or talk it out with me. I finally sat with Suzy at lunch and that was better."

"That was good. It's better to have more than one friend."

"I was mad at Sally. So I wanted to get back at her. Jake had asked me whether he could get a job at the store. I told my dad he'd be a good worker."

"From everything I've heard he is a good worker."

"Yeah, he is." I had slurped the last of my malt. I put the cup on the ground.

"Here, Colette." Aunt Florence held out her hand. I gave her the empty cup. "Why don't we walk?"

We both stood up. Aunt Florence put our empty cups in the trash bin. I liked the walk along the River Drive. It felt good to move around.

"Did anything else happen with Jake?"

"Yes, but I don't know if I can talk about it."

"Take your time, Colette. Remember what I said about a big weight coming off when I talked about Daniel."

I thought, what do I have to lose? I told her about accidentally meeting Jake and his friends in front of Musolf's. The words tumbled out of my mouth, one after another, to the point where I didn't even know what I was going to say next. Aunt Florence didn't say a word. "So we met outside and they all emptied their pockets of things they had stolen. I couldn't believe it. I was going to tell Tommy Musolf."

"Okay. I still don't understand what you did."

"Jake told me to empty my pockets and he had put a candy bar in there."

"Again. You didn't do it."

"I know but I didn't tell Tommy either. And on the way home, I ate the candy."

"So you felt guilty."

"Mr. Musolf was at our house sitting with Gramps when I got home. I went upstairs instead of talking with them. I didn't want Mr. Musolf and Gramps to know what I did. I felt terrible." I felt the tears in my eyes sting. I blinked hard.

Aunt Florence had her hands behind her back. She didn't interrupt.

"I guess I was embarrassed by the whole thing. I never thought that I wouldn't stand up to someone, especially when I knew it was wrong."

"Do a lot of people follow Jake?"

"Yeah. Everybody thinks he's cool. He has his own car and he's the star pitcher on the baseball team so the boys follow him. The girls think he's cute."

"He is a good-looking boy."

I remembered how I used to turn red whenever Jake looked at me or talked to me. He must have seen that. He would smile at me and get me to check out cigarettes for him, another thing I wasn't supposed to do. Now that I thought about it, I felt used. Really used.

"I have a question. Did you know he was stealing when you recommended him to your dad?"

Now I was really sad. Sometimes if I closed my eyelids tight, I could keep the tears from escaping. Aunt Florence had her arm around me. "It's okay." She steered me back to the benches around the Monument. The tears ran down my cheeks. Aunt Florence gave me some tissues; she always had some in her pocket. "I was just so dumb. I can't believe how dumb I was."

"People do a lot of things when they're hurt. You were very hurt by Sally. And I think you did kind of like Jake, didn't you?"

"I liked him paying attention to me. The girls at school seemed surprised when he talked to me at school. So it made me feel good, specially if Sally saw it."

"Completely understandable. Don't be so hard on yourself."

"So he started working at the store and then I was worried about his friends coming in and stealing from us. I checked out cigarettes for him and I wasn't supposed to. He knew I wouldn't say anything just like when he stole from Musolf's. And the whiskey too; he knew I wouldn't tell."

"Tell me about why you went to the party."

198

"I was furious at Jake after the whiskey deal. So I didn't talk to him at school. I worked with him yesterday. I tried to stay away from him all day. He invited me to the party before he left. I said no, I wasn't interested."

"Why did you change your mind?"

"I told Suzy about Jake taking the whiskey and then filling the bottle with water. Suzy started talking about how conceited Jake was. I found out she had been invited to the party by Sam. She said she knew the parents were gone so there'd be a lot of drinking. I got really worried about Sally because she didn't drink."

"So you went over there."

"I did. There were lots of kids there. I tried to get Sally to leave. She wouldn't. I was going to go home when the neighbor called and Jake told everyone to leave. That's when I brought Sally over to your house."

"Sally was lucky you went over there. Particularly after the way she treated you."

"I hope she didn't get in too much trouble."

"Colette, you're a good friend."

"Sally and I were best friends from first grade on. We had never had a fight. I hope we can talk it out and be friends again."

"I hope so too. Don't forget about Suzy."

"Suzy's really nice. I didn't pay any attention to her when I was with Sally. I'm not going to dump her now."

Aunt Florence nodded. "Feel better?"

"Yeah, I feel better."

"Do you have anything else to tell me about?"

"No."

"Okay, good. I'm going to tell you what I think. You didn't do anything wrong when it came to the movie other than being part of a lie. The incident at Musolf's was not your fault but you should have told Tommy about it. Jake coming over to our house was really inexcusable. I think he knew he had control over you and he wanted to see if you would tell on him."

"Maybe."

"The biggest problem with all that happened is the fact that you lied to your parents several times."

I didn't know what to say because it was true. I had lied; for Sally and for Jake. "What's going to happen now? Am I going to be grounded again?"

"I don't know what your parents will decide. I'll tell them what you told me. But you need to talk to them."

"Yeah, I know that."

"Why don't we drive back to Red Wing? I told your mother you'd be home in time for dinner."

Chapter Twenty Seven
Home Again

We drove back to Red Wing. I didn't want to talk anymore about Jake, Sally, or anything else for that matter.

"Tired?" Aunt Florence asked.

"Kind of. Thanks for everything today." Actually, I was exhausted. I closed my eyes.

"You're welcome. How about some music?" Aunt Florence turned on the radio. She found a station with a lot of her favorite Motown songs on it. She started singing. I couldn't help joining in since I loved the music too. The two of us sang all the way back to Red Wing.

We pulled up to my house. Uncle Mike's car was there. Great. The whole family would be staring at me and questioning me. I didn't want to go in.

"What's the matter?" Aunt Florence asked.

"I don't want everyone questioning me."

"Go sit with Gramps. He always watches sports on Sunday afternoon. I bet Rosie is with him too. I'll talk to your parents. Now, give me a hug."

I hugged Aunt Florence. She whispered, "It'll be all right."

My parents waited at the door. "Why don't we go into the kitchen?" Aunt Florence said. I walked into the living room. Gramps and Uncle Mike had the TV on to Wide World of Sports. Rosie was on Gramp's lap with a book open. "Rosie's been waiting for you," Gramps said. "Sit down."

"How was your day?" Gramps asked.

I could just say fine and Gramps wouldn't ask any more questions or I could go into a lot of details and he would listen. That's the way he was. "Well, we ate at the River Room."

"Did you have popovers?"

"Yes. And chicken pot pie. I have to say that Aunt Florence puts more butter on her popovers than anyone except you, Gramps." Gramps absolutely loved to talk about food.

"Nothing like melted butter."

"Then we got strawberry malts at the Dairy Queen and went to the Monument to eat them."

"Sounds good. Did you do anything else?"

"We talked. Aunt Florence and I talked."

"Was that good?"

"Yes. It was good."

Uncle Mike hadn't said anything. He kept looking toward the kitchen. I suppose he wondered what Aunt Florence was saying to my parents. I did too for that matter. I thought of taking Rosie outside but I didn't know if Uncle Mike would want me to. Anyway, Gramps loved every minute he had with little Rosie.

Aunt Florence came out of the kitchen. She looked at me and smiled so I guess that was a good sign. "Mike, what are you thinking for dinner?"

"I don't know. Should we take Rosie out?"

"I think so. That would be fun." Aunt Florence, Mike, and Rosie left. Gramps went outside with them.

My mother came out of the kitchen. She crooked her finger to me. "Florence told us what happened with the movie and Musolf's."

"I'm going to fire Jake," my dad said.

I took in a deep breath. "Sorry that I recommended him."

"I'm not going to have someone who steals working for me."

"That's for sure," my mom said. "I knew you hadn't taken the whiskey but I didn't know what happened."

I wanted to say; then why was I grounded for so long?

"The party could have been a disaster. By the way, don't the boys and girls on the teams say they won't drink?"

"They can be kicked off the team. The whole baseball team was there. I think they're lucky the neighbor called."

"They're finishing up the season too. When's their last game?"

My mom was making small talk, so she couldn't be all that mad at me. "Friday."

"And yours is Saturday."

"We wish you wouldn't have lied to us," my dad said. "If you had told us about Musolf's, a lot of this would have been avoided."

"I know that now. Am I going to be grounded again?" My fingers were crossed behind my back.

My mom chimed in. "As much as I love having you help me in the kitchen, I think you need to go to softball practice." She looked over at my dad. "And with this being my last week at St. Anastasia's, I just can't take any more drama."

"What does that mean?" My dad said.

"I mean I don't think Colette should be grounded. She was helping Sally. She wasn't drinking."

My fingers were still crossed. One thing I had noticed through the years was that if my parents disagreed, which was rare, my mom usually won.

"I think we should eat," my mom said. "Then your dad and I will discuss this whole situation."

At dinner, Gramps asked me all about St. Paul. I told them about driving down Summit Avenue and how Aunt Florence knew so much history. She talked about James J. Hill and the Great Northern Railway; the James J. Hill house was huge. She pointed out a house that had a little square on the top. She said that you could see when the boats came down the river from the little room and that's what it was for. She got really excited about a house where a famous author had lived. His last name was Fitzgerald and he wrote a book I hadn't read. Aunt Florence knew all about him and she assured me I'd be reading his books in the future.

Gramps talked about what he liked about Summit Avenue in St. Paul. It helped pass the time at dinner.

My dad helped my mom clean up on Sundays so they both went into the kitchen. I went to the living room where Gramps was already sitting. I knew my parents weren't done with me yet and they would want to hear my side of the story.

Gramps liked to watch Perry Mason on Sunday nights. Once it started you couldn't talk at all. It was starting in a half hour so Gramps and I would have some quiet before Perry got Gramp's full attention.

"What do you want to talk about?" Gramps asked.

"I don't know."

"I'm only going to ask you one question, Bella. Were you able to talk to Florence?"

"Yes."

"Maybe someday you'll talk to me about it. Should we talk about softball?"

"Sure, Gramps." So we talked about hot grounders, line drives, and stealing bases until Perry Mason started.

"Colette," my mom called.

"Coming." I walked to the kitchen.

"Your dad and I have decided no grounding."

"Thank you."

"No more lying, Colette," my dad said.

"I won't."

"Okay. I'm going to give Jake a call." He went into the sunroom so he could have some privacy. He wasn't gone more than five minutes. "That's done," he said.

"What did he say?"

"He asked if it was about the party. I said no, there were other things. He asked if I wasn't happy with his work. I said no, he did a good job but we couldn't trust him after hearing about stealing from Musolf's and Mike's whiskey. He seemed kind of shocked. Then I said I didn't like him intimidating you so he was fired."

I don't know why but I felt kind of sorry for Jake.

"You're going to have to work every Saturday for a while," my mom said.

"I can do that. What about the big game?"

"I'm going to close the store for a half day." my dad said. Maybe my dad had listened to Gramps about spending more time with the family. "I only have one kid and I want to see the championship game."

Chapter Twenty Eight
The Big Game

It was a relief to tell Aunt Florence about everything that had happened. My parents and I came to an understanding while Gramps was watching Perry Mason. They had many questions and I told them the whole story.

On Monday, I met Suzy in the cafeteria about ten minutes before school started. I told her about the party and why I left her house so quickly. She said she understood and she wasn't one bit surprised about how crazy the party was.

Sam was furious with me for taking Sally away from the party and over to Aunt Florence's. At school on Monday, Sally thanked me again for getting her away from the party. She told me both she and John were grounded for a week but John could play baseball. She walked away from Sam when Sam tried to talk to her in homeroom. She said we would have to talk things out in the next week.

At practice, everybody on the team was happy to see me. Everyone, that is, except Sam O'Malley.

"Let's line up for batting practice," Coach Richter said. "O'Malley, you can pitch."

It felt good to stand at home plate again. I took a couple of swings. I was ready. Sam wound up and hit me right on my left hip. I yelped, believe me. I went down in the dirt.

Coach Richter went crazy. He raced up to the pitcher's mound, took Sam's glove, threw it on the ground, and yelled loud enough for people strolling down Main Street to hear. Nobody moved, including Sam O'Malley.

"What was that? You trying to hurt her?" He screamed. From home plate I could see the spit flying. "I asked you a question, O'Malley."

"I just lost control, Coach. I don't know what happened."

"Go sit on the bench for the rest of practice."

Sam walked toward the bench. I stood at home plate, rubbing my hip. It really hurt. Several girls surrounded me, asking if I was okay. Suzy stood right next to me and kept patting my arm. Sam walked by in a huff.

"Excuse me," Coach Richter said. "You forgot something."

Sam kept walking.

"Didn't you hear me? Apologize to McGiver right now."

"I'm sorry," Sam said without even turning around.

"I'm going to tell you something. You either apologize or you're not playing in the championship game."

That got her attention. She turned around. "I'm really sorry, Colette."

"I'm talking to everyone now. If you have problems with each other for whatever reason, leave it off the field. It doesn't belong here. We're a team and we work together." Coach Richter paced back and forth. He walked over to the cooler he always brought with him. He took out a plastic bag and put ice in it. He wrapped it in a small towel. "Here, McGiver. Stay put. No running." He handed me the ice. "Okay, let's continue batting practice."

Sam stood up from the bench, picked up her glove, and headed toward the mound.

"I guess you didn't hear me, O'Malley. I said sit on the bench and be quiet. McGough, you pitch practice today."

McGough ran to the pitching mound. Sam threw her glove on the ground and sat back on the bench. I sat as far over on the opposite end as I could from Sam. I didn't look at her. I put the ice on my hip and watched practice.

My parents and Gramps were really mad at Sam. My mom made me put more ice on my hip. "How are you supposed to play on Saturday?"

"I'm playing. And I'm going to practice tomorrow too." I didn't say anything about the grounding because my mom and dad knew they had overreacted and I knew that I had lied several times. I guess we were both wrong.

On Friday, I was glad to say goodbye to all the teachers at City Bluffs since summer was my favorite time of the year. Not only could I sleep late, read only what I wanted to, listen to music to my heart's content, but I didn't have to write any papers or do any homework. The other great thing about summer was I could put on my shorts and a shirt, ride my bike all over town, go walk by the river, check out Musolf's new merchandise; all while enjoying the green trees and the blue, blue sky of Minnesota.

The championship game was at ten o'clock on Saturday in Lake City. Mr. Musolf, Oma, and Tommy were going to the game, but Musolf's would be open so Fred couldn't come. Tommy had talked to me about the candy bar. I told him I hoped we could still be friends. He said, "My whole family is friends with your whole family so we're friends too."

The drive down to Lake City was really pretty. Gramps exclaimed as soon as Lake Pepin came into view. He told us, as he always did, about the Sunday drives he used to take with Grandma Rose, my mom, Uncle Daniel, and Aunt Florence. "Look for eagles," Gramps said happily.

We were at the softball field by nine o'clock. Most of the girls were already there. Coach Richter was talking to the umpire and the other coach. He came over to the bench. "Okay, girls, we can have the field in fifteen minutes for a quick warm-up. Just relax, for now."

My hip ached but not like the beginning of the week. The only problem was running really hard. The coach told me he wouldn't give me the signal to steal but it was my decision if I thought it was a good move.

Coach Richter said, "Gather round, girls. We're here today because of your hard work. I've enjoyed every minute of coaching you. I know you'll give your best like you always do but have fun too. Okay, quick prayer." He bowed his head, "Thank you, Lord, for all your blessings. Our Father who art in heaven..." We all joined in with our hands in the center.

Aunt Florence, Uncle Mike, and Rosie waved from the stands. Sally and Mrs. Reynolds were there too. Mrs. Reynolds had talked to my mom about the movie and the party. She decided she should spend more time with Sally alone.

I was the number one batter so I started the game. "Okay, girls, talk it up," Coach Richter said.

"C'mon, Colette."

"Start us off."

"Wait for your pitch."

The first pitch was right over the plate. I didn't swing. I waited for the next pitch. It was outside. One strike, one ball. I dug in by the plate, took a couple of swings, and waited. The pitch came in waist high. I stepped into the pitch and swung as hard as I could. Crack! It was a hot grounder between the shortstop and second base. I was on first.

I looked over at the coach and then remembered that I could decide if I wanted to steal or not. Donahue was batting. I knew she would swing if the ball was anywhere near the strike zone because she was so afraid of a called strike. Donahue swung at the first pitch and hit a little dribbler to the pitcher. The pitcher scooped it up and threw it to the second baseman. I was out and Donahue was out on a double play. Sam O'Malley batted third. She was really good when runners were on base. She stepped into the pitch and hit a long fly ball to center field. Lake City's center fielder caught it. No problem. Our side was out.

"Okay. Shake it off," Coach Richter said. "We've got six more innings."

We ran out to our positions. Lake City's first batter hit a pop up to Sheila Donahue on first. One out. The second batter hit down the third base line. I charged it and threw it to first. Two outs. The third batter struck out. Three outs. Our turn at bat.

The game was like the first inning with both teams struggling to even get a batter on base. It was a pitcher's duel like our first game. I was glad Sam was on our team even though she wasn't talking to me. She struck out more batters than the Lake City pitcher.

I got on base to start out the fifth inning. I decided to try to steal on the next pitch. The second their pitcher released the ball, I raced toward second. Donahue swung and missed. I was on second and in scoring position. Donahue grounded to the shortstop who waited to hold me at second before throwing it to first. Donahue was out. Sam O'Malley stood at the plate. She moved her feet around in the dirt and swung a couple of times. Sam didn't like to swing at the first pitch so I waited.

Since we didn't have any runs, if the ball was hit out of the infield, Coach Richter would be waving me home. My hip still hurt a little bit but I had stolen second with no problem.

The pitcher wound up and threw. Crack! Sam hit a line drive that whizzed by me into center field. I was off. The coach screamed, "Go home, McGiver. Go home." I didn't slow down to see where the ball was.

Their center fielder rifled the ball to the shortstop who was the cutoff person. The people in the stands were standing so I knew it was close. I couldn't run any faster. We didn't slide like the boys and the catcher couldn't block home plate. Their catcher was in front of the base. I was about five feet away. The shortstop hurled the ball toward home. I heard the smack of the ball in the catcher's glove. I went around the back of the base as the catcher spun around trying to tag me. I got my toe on the base.

"Safe," the umpire yelled.

Our whole bench had been standing. Now they were cheering, clapping, and slapping me on the back. The score was 1-0. Sam O'Malley waited on second hoping to score too. The next two batters both struck out.

Lake City's first batter didn't waste any time. She swung at the first pitch and she was off toward first base. The ball streaked down the third base line. I had to back hand the ball to keep it from going into left field. I threw to first. It landed in the dirt and Donahue couldn't handle it. The runner raced toward second. Their next batter hit the ball to first. One out but they had a runner on third.

Sam wound up. The batter smashed the ball to right field. The right fielder waited and caught the ball on the fly. Two outs but the runner on third tagged up and scored. It was 1-1. The next batter dribbled the ball to Sam who scooped it up and threw it to first. Three outs.

Our turn to bat. Laurie Zastrow got ready. She swung twice and missed. The next four pitches were balls. Zastrow was on first. The next pitch she took off for second. The hit and run play told the batter to swing if someone was stealing. Our batter swung hard. The catcher bobbled the ball. Zastrow was safe at second. Pearson struck out. The coach told Suzy just to get Zastrow to third. She did more than that. She hit a line drive right up the middle. Zastrow ran toward third. The coach waved her toward home. We were all standing and yelling. The ball came home right after Zastrow scored. It was 2-1. Suzy decided to run toward third. Their catcher quickly threw to third. Suzy was out. The next batter hit a pop up to the shortstop. Our side was out.

"Hold them now," Coach Richter said.

It was the bottom of the seventh inning. Lake City had runners on first and second. The batter swung hard and smashed it. The ball was a high line drive to second. It looked like it would easily land in center field. Both runners left their bases. Zastrow leapt straight up, stabbed the ball out of the air, pivoted around, and ran toward the base runner who had left first, tagged her out, pivoted around again, and ran toward second. The runner who had been racing back to second, turned around, and ran toward third. Zastrow threw it to me. The batter was in the hotbox. I threw to Zastrow who moved toward the runner. The runner ran toward third. Zastrow threw the ball to me while moving closer to third. I ran after the runner and tagged her out. Triple play!

Well, I tell you, we went nuts. Laurie Zastrow looked like the Cheshire Cat, her smile was so wide. We circled around her and pounded her on the back. The coach had leapt off the bench and run to second. "That was exciting," he said. "Thank you to all of you for a great season. Have a good summer. Go line up and shake Lake City's hands."

"Good game."

"Good game."

Mrs. Reynolds and my mom were having a discussion. They looked really serious. Sally came over and said, "We have to talk. How about tomorrow afternoon?"

"At your house?"

"Yeah. One o'clock?"

"Okay. I've gotta go." As much as I wanted to talk things out with Sally, I felt a little nervous. After all, she stopped talking to me for months over something we should have been able to work out. I was glad I got her away from the party but I wasn't going to get my hopes up about our relationship. I guess I didn't trust her not to dump me again.

Aunt Florence, Uncle Mike, Rosie, my parents, Gramps, and the Musolfs waited by the stands for me. Aunt Florence loved to scream and cheer at games so her voice was husky when she said, "That was great. Congratulations."

"It was a great game, wasn't it?" I said.

Chapter Twenty Nine
A Talk with Sally

On the ride home, Gramps went over the plays of the last two innings again and again. I wish I could have recreated the triple play; it was so wonderful.

My dad opened the store at two o'clock and my mom went with him. Gramps and I had the afternoon to ourselves. I told him the story of Jake from beginning to end. He listened intently. He commented, "You've learned a valuable lesson. I hope you remember that lies might start out small but they always multiply."

"I will."

"You know your family loves you. You can tell us anything," he said.

Easier said than done. There were some things I couldn't tell my family. That's why I needed a best friend. I didn't want Gramps to worry about me. "I know I can talk to you," I said.

The next day, we walked to nine o'clock Mass as usual. We went to the Diner for breakfast as usual. Gramps got his pancakes and exclaimed as usual. I got my eggs, over hard, and hash browns as usual. It was a usual kind of morning.

The afternoon would be far from usual. I hadn't been over at Sally's house for almost three months. I tried not to expect too much.

I rode my bike over to Sally's. She opened the door before I rang the bell. "C'mon in. We'll go up to my room."

Mrs. Reynolds said, "Good to see you, Colette."

She couldn't be too mad at me. "Good to see you too," I said.

We went up to Sally's room. "Just a minute," she said. She checked the closet for stray ears in the form of Anna or Margaret. "It's clear," she said. "Sit down."

I sat on the bed her two sisters shared. She sat on her bed and leaned forward toward me. "Thanks again, Colette, for saving me at that party. My mom said that could have been really bad for me. She went on and on about what happens when kids are drinking and no parents are around."

"That's why I went there."

"You're a lot smarter than me. By the way, did you hear that Jake's parents were really mad too?"

"I heard his parents took his car away."

"I heard that too."

The conversation was hardly moving along quickly. There were lapses of silence and I wondered if Sally and I would be okay.

"Anyway, John and I are not allowed to be with the O'Malleys. My mom said that Jake is a wild boy and she was right about him from the beginning."

Now, this was something new.

"She said she doesn't like Sam either. So they're both banned from our house."

I wondered if Sally was worried about a long summer without anybody to talk to. I chose not to think that was the only reason she was talking to me. My mom told me to keep an open mind. Still, she had never apologized for not talking to me.

Sally was biting her nails so I knew she was nervous. "This is so hard, Colette. I never thought we'd have trouble talking with each other."

That was it. "That's what happens when you don't talk to someone for months. And when you don't want them at the lunch table. And when you blame them for your date that wasn't a date. Maybe we don't have much to say to each other." I stood up and walked toward the door. "I should go," I said.

"Please don't go. I apologize for that whole movie mess. I am truly sorry for acting so crazy that night."

"Why did you give me the silent treatment?"

"I don't know. I was mad, I guess."

My hand was still on the doorknob. "I know how stubborn and proud you are, Sally, but that really hurt my feelings."

Sally walked over to me. She put her arms around me. "Colette, I understand if you don't want to be my friend anymore. In fact, I deserve it. I'm sorry for hurting your feelings. Please believe me."

I didn't want to cry but I couldn't help it. Sally started crying too. We hugged. "Should we sit down again?" She said.

Sally gave me a tissue. I wiped my eyes. She gave me another tissue. I blew my nose. "Well, this is a new one. The two of us crying up in my bedroom." She giggled.

I laughed. "Maybe we should do this more often."

"Once a month, I'd say."

I missed this; the laughter. It seemed like Sally did feel bad about not talking to me. I guess that was a start. "I have something to tell you that might actually shock you."

"What? Tell me."

Here goes, I thought. I told Sally about Musolf's. She put her hand over her mouth.

"John did that?" Sally asked. "I can't believe it."

"John and Mike too. Jake was the organizer."

"Wow. That happened the day after the movie?"

"Yeah. The day after."

"Why didn't you tell Tommy Musolf?"

"I don't know. I was embarrassed. I didn't want to be a tattletale. So I ate the candy bar on the way home."

Sally was leaning forward at this point. "Colette, you didn't steal it."

"I felt so bad when I got home and saw Mr. Musolf. I didn't know what to do."

"Then what happened?"

"Jake started working at our store." I told her about checking out cigarettes for him. "I didn't like having him there after awhile. Then he came over when I was babysitting one night." I told her about the whiskey. "So that's it. That's why I knew I had to go to that party."

"All I have to say is that Jake is a bully. Is that why you were grounded?"

"Yes, I was accused of taking the whiskey."

"You didn't tell the truth?"

"No."

"You didn't tell on me either about the movie or the party."

"No, I didn't."

"Thanks, Colette. I really was obsessed with Jake. I wanted to blame you for the fact that he wasn't interested. I'm lucky he wasn't."

"Sally," Mrs. Reynolds yelled. She opened the door. "It's four o'clock. I need to run to the store. Please babysit for an hour at the most."

"I'll be right down," she said. "Gotta go, Colette. Thank you for talking to me."

"Sure."

I hadn't told Sally about going up to St. Paul with Aunt Florence. Or about Jake being fired. We had lots more to talk about.

Sally told her parents about Musolf's. Mrs. Reynolds took John to Musolf's and made him apologize. He had to give them ten dollars. She asked him if that was the only time they had stolen. John didn't answer. Mr. Reynolds got involved then. John was grounded for two weeks. He couldn't drive for a month. He had to do all the yard work and Mrs. Reynolds had him babysitting which Sally loved.

I felt more and more comfortable talking to Sally again. I didn't see any reason to stay mad. I remembered what Aunt Florence said about Suzy. I told Sally that Suzy was my friend too. If she wanted to be friends again, Suzy was included. She agreed.

Chapter Thirty
Jake Falls

On July third, Sally, Suzy, and I went for a long bike ride after dinner. The downtown was really busy because all the stores were closed on the Fourth. So we decided to go north of downtown until we got tired. At this time of year it was still light until almost ten o'clock. We talked as we rode.

Sally was very chatty about her brother, John, and all the work he had had to do in the last couple of weeks. "I wanted to cheer when my dad said he had to cut the grass."

"Doesn't he do that anyway?" Suzy asked.

"John? Ha. He's an expert at being gone when my parents need a babysitter or the grass needs cutting."

"We have jobs we have to do first before going anywhere," Suzy said. "Like I have to dust every Saturday. One of my brothers cleans the kitchen floor. The other one always helps with the trash. Plus we have to clean our rooms."

"I refuse to clean my room because there are three of us in the room."

"You poor thing," Suzy said.

"I know. My sister, Anna, is really messy. She can never find her clothes because they're all over the floor. It's a total disaster. Isn't it, Colette?"

"Yeah. It's unbelievable. By the way, is John mad at me?" I asked.

"Who cares? He's the one who was stealing. Tonight John is staying overnight at Mike's house. He couldn't wait to get out of the house."

Boom!

"What do you think that is?" Suzy asked.

"I don't know. Whatever it is, it's pretty big." The sounds continued. Boom! Boom!

"Let's go see who's there," Sally said. She turned her bike towards the river.

Red Wing had lots of parks and some of them were on the river. There was one my mom called Party Park because kids liked to go there to hang out, drink, and party. Every summer kids would be partying and someone would fall into the river. My mom made me promise never to go there.

"I'm not supposed to go to Party Park," I said.

"C'mon, Colette," Sally said.

"I don't know. I've gotten in enough trouble this summer already." I stood by my bike. Boom! It was definitely coming from the river. "Suzy, what do you think?"

"I wonder who's down there and what they're doing. Don't you?"

"I guess. Okay, let's go." It was eight thirty but still light so we headed down to the river. It didn't take us long to find the source of the noise. Jake, John, Mike, and a few other kids had a fire going. They were lighting off firecrackers, actually M-80's, from sticks they pulled out of the fire. One person lit it and then ran. Everybody stayed far away from the M-80's. Boom!

"Well, look who's here," Jake said. "I suppose you want to tell on me again." There was no smile on his face and his blue eyes were cold and icy. "Get lost."

I shivered. I couldn't think of anything to say.

"John, you're not supposed to be with Jake," Sally said.

"And you're not supposed to be down here. So just be quiet."

Sally looked like she wanted to say something but she saw Sam and waved to her. I felt more and more uncomfortable. I had nothing to say to anyone. I stood by Suzy. "I'm ready to leave. How about you?"

"I don't need to stay any longer," Suzy said.

"Let's ask Sally what she thinks," I said. Sally was in an animated conversation with Sam. "We'll wait until Sally wants to go. Please stick by me, Suzy."

Suzy gave my arm a quick squeeze.

"Watch this," Jake said. Jake took his cigarette out of his mouth, put the lit end on the little fuse, and threw the M-80 up into the air. Boom! "Not much room to spare that time," he said.

"That's really dangerous, Jake," Sam said. "You could blow off your fingers. What's the matter with you?"

"That didn't happen."

"I said it could happen. Just think, you wouldn't be able to play football or baseball anymore."

"Settle down, Sis. Nothing happened."

"Quit being such a show-off."

John and Mike looked at each other. "I'm going home," Mike said.

"Me too," John said.

"Okay, okay. I'm just having a little fun." Jake backed up away from the fire. He was right on the edge of the river.

Sally came over by Suzy and me. She whispered, "Let's go."

"If Jake gets any closer, he's going to fall in," I said.

"Oh well," Sally said. "I never realized how stupid he is."

We heard a splash and turned. Jake had fallen backwards into the river. He yelled, "Help, I can't swim." His legs and arms flailed and his head went under water. Everyone ran over. His head came up and he screeched, "Help me."

The water didn't seem deep but the river could be deceiving. I wondered if he could stand. "Stand up. Just stand up," I yelled.

Jake thrashed like a turtle on its back. He shrieked, "I'm drowning."

John, Mike, and Sam shouted, "Stand up. You can stand. It's only two feet deep."

"Maybe he's really in trouble," I said.

John and Mike walked into the water. "C'mon, man, stand up," Mike said. Each of them grabbed one of Jake's arms and pulled him up. He stood shakily at first and then caught his footing. The water came to his knees. He walked out of the river, completely drenched. I held out my hand. He batted it away. "I was kidding," he said. He ran his fingers through his hair.

"Right, you were kidding." Sam said. She slapped his arm.

Mike and John laughed out loud. John said, "You were scared. No big deal."

"You can't be serious," Jake said. "I fooled all of you."

"You sure did," Sally said.

"I wasn't scared," Jake said. "I was just having some fun."

"Okay. Whatever you say," Sally said. She patted me on the back. "Should we go?"

Sam stopped us. "I shouldn't have been so mean," she said. "Sorry."

We walked over to our bikes. Suzy was almost jumping up and down. "I'm so glad we went there. Jake was screaming when all he had to do was stand up."

"He was panicking, that's for sure. I knew the water wasn't deep there. It was only funny because it was Jake. I'm glad he's okay." I got on my bike. "It's getting dark. Let's go."

"I can't believe I liked him," Sally said.

"I can't either," Suzy said. "I knew he was a phony from the first time I saw him."

"You were smarter than me," Sally said. "Are we meeting for the fireworks tomorrow?"

"Good idea," I said.

"I'm in," said Suzy.

I didn't tell my parents about the events at the river that night but I did the next day. One of the promises I had made to myself was that I would not lie to my family. I thought I might get into trouble for going down to the river but I had learned that I wasn't the type of person who could hold things in. So I told my mom, dad, and Gramps at breakfast. They couldn't believe it.

"Were you in any danger?" my mom asked.

"No, mom, I really wasn't." I quickly added, "I know the river can be dangerous and I'm really careful."

"I don't think you should make this a habit. I mean hanging out at the river," my dad said.

"I won't."

Gramps had been sitting with his hands on his lap. "That was quite a story. I'm glad you noticed he was in trouble. I can't swim either so that might have been my reaction."

So that's my story. Jake apologized to my dad for everything that had gone on with me. He went to Musolf's and apologized to all of them. He even apologized to Mrs. Reynolds. I guess once he started he just kept apologizing. My mom said he must have been thinking about all the things he did, so maybe landing in the river was good for him.

Sam apologized to Mrs. Reynolds for the party. Sam also apologized to me for hitting me at practice. I told her I had already forgotten about it. After the apologies, Mrs. Reynolds told John and Sally that they could see Jake and Sam. She made them promise that there wouldn't be any more "shenanigans."

I guess I'm a pretty lucky girl. Sophomore year will be starting in a couple weeks. I'll be trying out for the varsity basketball team and I hope I make it. Sally, Suzy, Sam, and I hope to have the same homeroom again and maybe some classes together. We decided we won't keep secrets from each other. And we'll never ever get mad at each other. I'll keep my fingers crossed.

I tell Aunt Florence every couple of weeks that she's my favorite aunt. She acts surprised and then says, "Wait a minute. I'm your only one." She says we should go to the River Room and St. Paul when we don't need to have a heart-to-heart. Just for the fun of it. She plans on coming to all my basketball games with little Rosie. Uncle Mike told me he was wrong to get so mad at me and I could babysit anytime.

My cousin, Daniel, came to Red Wing for a visit before he went back to Madison. I told him about Jake, the movie, Sally not talking to me, Musolf's, the whiskey, the party, and finally the firecrackers and Jake falling in the river. Daniel listened to the whole story. He said, "Jake isn't so cool after all."

Next week we're going to Lake Itasca for four nights. I can't wait. And, my dad said, we can go to the North Shore next summer so we can be in awe of Lake Superior. I can't wait for that either. I'm trying to convince Gramps that we should go to Italy at Christmas. He didn't say no.

My mom's happy she won't be working at St. Anastasia's in the fall. She said it was too much with both school and the store. My dad said he isn't so worried about expanding the business anymore. He said in a couple years I'll be away at college so he doesn't want to miss any games or anything else I'm doing.

And Gramps. What can I say about him? He's perfect just the way he is.

About the Author

Mary Clare is a retired Oncology / Hospice RN. She has a BA in Creative Writing from Metropolitan State University. Her stories have appeared in several Chicken Soup books, various magazines, and Handprints on My Heart on-line. She has written  three other books: *Warning! Family Vacations May Be Hazardous to Your Health, Barefoot, Shoefoot,* and *They're Always With You. They're Always With You* won the 2014 Midwest Book Award for Young Adult Fiction. She has four daughters, four sons-in-law, and six grand-children. She has been married to Paul for thirty nine years.

If you like the book, a positive review on Amazon.com would be helpful.